Please feel free to send me an email. J
these emails. Good news is always we

Sabrina Noury - sabrina_noury@aweso........

Sign up for my blog for updates and freebies!
http://sabrina-noury.awesomeauthors.org

About the Publisher

BLVNP Incorporated, A Nevada Corporation, 340 S. Lemon #6200, Walnut CA 91789, info@blvnp.com / legal@blvnp.com

DISCLAIMER

Silent Luna

By: Sabrina Noury

ISBN: 978-1-68030-929-4

Table of Contents

For Grammy,

"Anyone who ever gave you confidence, you owe them a lot"
Breakfast at Tiffany's

FREE DOWNLOAD

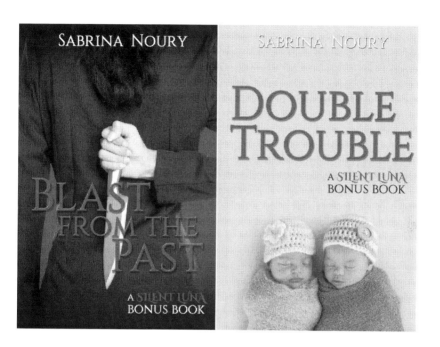

Get these freebies and MORE when you sign up for the author's mailing list!

sabrina_noury@awesomeauthors.org

Chapter 1

I have thought about my death for the better majority of my life. I had thought about how I would die, who or what would kill me, and how much time I had before it happened.

For a long time, it was an obsession, something I could not stop thinking about day in and day out. It was always hanging over my head, always lurking around some corner.

The only thing I thought about more than my death was that I would never get to see my family again. I couldn't watch my sister grow up, go to school, and eventually, get married. I wouldn't be there to take care of my parents when they got old and sick. I wouldn't be able to get married one day myself and have children of my own.

I would miss all of that because of someone else.

One day, I was so consumed with the fact that my entire life had been taken away from me, that I just lost control.

Then I escaped.

***

For an infinite amount of time, it felt like all I could do was run. One foot in front of the other and just keep pushing. I know that eventually, my body would give out, but the second I stopped, I know I would be in trouble.

Not the kind of trouble that would be manageable, but the kind of trouble that would get me killed.

If I am going to die, I don't want to give them the satisfaction of doing it. The pain along my leg had gone numb a long time ago, but I am just now starting to feel the blood loss and exhaustion hitting me. I sit down next to a tree to take a break and just think about my life.

I was eight when I was taken. There was an attack in the middle of the night, and nobody saw it coming because we were at peace with all of our allies.

I am a werewolf, and in the werewolf community, it is always important to have allies. A pack can be very large, but they can't defend themselves from everything. Since I was so young, I had never shifted before. This meant I could not defend myself against any of the shifted wolves around me. I was an easy prey.

After I had been taken away from the pack and my family, we traveled for a long time. The first couple of days were very hazy, and I had no idea what was going on. After a couple of years, it was a daily routine for them to keep me to do their chores, make their food, and to take their frustrations out on when life go too hard.

I could barely remember my old life after a year or two.

Almost ten years later, I have managed to escape, and now I have no idea where to go or what to do. They could be right on my trail for all I know, and then the fight and me finally shifting into my wolf were all for nothing.

Ever since they took me, they tormented me and kept me for years now. I was supposed to cook for them and entertain them whenever they wanted.

But most of them were dead now, all except for their leader.

Realizing I can in no way go any farther and that I am not healing quickly enough, I accept my death. It is almost peaceful to think that after my life of torture, I can finally die peacefully. I lie down still in wolf form and curl up into a ball, waiting to die or possibly start to heal and gain some strength back.

About a half an hour later, I hear something walking in the woods. I stand up on all four legs and look around me. Suddenly, a huge brown wolf with a blond-tipped tail is staring back at me, looking fully prepared to kill me.

The wolf starts growling, and out of instinct, I crouch into a defensive position. I put my head down on my front paws and just watch him. He walks back and forth, and after finally deciding I am not going to attack him, he shifts back into his human form and puts some shorts on.

"Shift," the guy says. I put my ears down and whine a little. His strong voice scares me a bit, and I want to shift back, but that is difficult because I don't really know how.

I have been running around the woods for hours in my wolf form because I wasn't sure how to, and I am also faster this way.

When I shifted into a wolf, it was not on purpose, and I don't really know how it happened.

"SHIFT!" he says louder. I whine louder and put my head down. When he sees this, he squints and squats down.

"Have you ever shifted before?" I shake my head, and he sighs.

"Just think about yourself as a human, and you have to want to go back to that form."

I do what he says, picturing my long brown hair down to my waist, my petite 5-foot-tall figure, and my bright green eyes. Seconds later, I feel my bones morphing for the second time that day; it is less painful than the first time, but it still hurts. After I had shifted, I lie on the ground naked in a ball. Now back in my human form, I can see I have a huge gash on my upper thigh on my left leg all the way down to my ankle.

A few seconds later, I hear the big guy in front of me start to talk.

Chapter 2

"Our pack doctor is on his way and will be here any minute, and our Alpha will come after that. You aren't really on our territory yet for another quarter of a mile or so, but he will still want to question you." I just laid there listening, but as soon as he says others are coming, I start crawling away, fear gripping me.

Another group is going to kidnap me again.

Not again. Please not again. I think to myself.

I try getting up but quickly fall again when I can't hold myself up. The brunette comes to help me, but as soon as he starts stepping closer, I start scooting back on my butt using my arms.

Once he sees what I am doing, he stops and holds his hands up.

"I'm not going to hurt you okay? How about you tell me your name?" he asks. I just stare at him. Ten seconds later, an older man starts walking towards us. He has a shirt in his hands and is dressed in jeans and a regular t-shirt.

When the doctor starts coming towards me, he starts talking to the brunette at the same time.

"How did you meet her?" the doctor asks.

"I was on my way back to the territory when I found her lying here. She didn't know how to shift, but she is really hurt on her leg." They both turn to look at me, and I instantly freeze up again.

"I see," the doctor says. He looks towards me and at my leg, but when he starts walking closer, I start scooting away, silent tears running down my face. I didn't even notice I had been crying this entire time.

"Listen, you have to let me come look at your leg. It's really bad, and you may need stitches," he says, but I am barely listening.

My mind only thinks of how I can run away when I can't even stand up. He holds his hands up and gently throws the shirt towards me. I watch them warily as I put it on as quickly as I can. I am drowning in this shirt, but I am not surprised considering how small I am compared to them.

Once he sees me looking around, he nods at the brunette. "You are going to have to help me talk to her or calm her down. She seems young and frightened, and she needs medical attention immediately."

The other guy starts walking towards me, and I notice a third guy has arrived and is on his way to 'help.'

This guy is blond with blue eyes. He is taller, but not as tall as the brunette though both are built like fighters.

I don't say a word as I am struggling to crawl away and cry while the boys walk towards me. When they get to me, the brunette comes by my head and sits next to me, putting my upper body in front of him while the blond sits at my feet holding my legs. They try and reassure me that it's okay; they just need to look at my leg and that everything will be okay. I struggle for a couple of seconds, but I start to get tired and weary. I have lost a lot of blood by now, and I am guessing the only thing that has kept be running for the past hour or so is the adrenaline.

I just sag against them, crying a little louder now. The doctor looks at my leg and starts cleaning it up with a cloth and alcohol. I scream a little from the pain when I hear a growl from the woods behind me.

"Mine!" is all I hear. As soon as I hear his voice, I feel a little sliver of comfort. I have no idea why and then I start to get confused. The guys that are holding me go stiff and look up at the man. I look up too, and when I see him, I melt a little on the inside.

He is by far the most handsome person I have ever seen, and a tiny voice in my head is telling me to run to him. The new man easily is bigger than the other guys. Not only is he as tall as a mountain, but he is built beyond the two before. His muscles bulge out of his black V-neck, and his jeans fit him perfectly, not too tight but tight enough to see the defined muscles in his legs. When I realize I am checking him out, I look up to his chiseled face with his brunette hair that has that messy style sticking up in the front.

But when I look into his eyes, I am instantly more frightened of him than anyone else here. His eyes are what scare me the most. Right now, they are pitch black, staring directly at me.

Chapter 3

Right as I see those eyes, I try getting up to run away again, and then I remember that I am sandwiched between the other two beasts that are holding me down.

I start whimpering and crying very loudly now, struggling a lot harder to get out, and if by some miracle they actually let me go. When I start moving away, the doctor decides to pipe up.

"Alpha, they were trying to help me take care of her. We were unaware she is your mate," he says, bowing his head.

"Nobody touches my mate!" he yells. At this point, I am full on sobbing while trying unsuccessfully to stand.

In all my years at the cabin, it has been a long time since I cried this hard. Maybe it was getting my freedom back, only for it to be ripped away hours later, or the fact that my leg just started gushing blood again, or even because, despite the look on the big guy's face, I still had this feeling that he was safe.

"Sorry, Alpha," the others say in unison.

When I look at the big guy, he is starting to head towards me. I start screaming, and I try to stand, but I don't make it too far when two strong arms wrap around my waist.

"Where are you going, princess?" the big guy asks. As I feel his breath on my neck along with his voice, I feel a shiver run down my spine. The next thing I know, he spins me around and picks me up effortlessly bridal style.

I wish I could say it was easy because I wasn't fighting him, but I was fighting and squirming the whole time.

Not that it helped much.

Even struggling as hard as I am, there is no point. This man is well over a foot taller than me, has the body of a god, and looks like he works out every day, all day. While I am sitting here barely over five feet tall, bleeding, and who knows the last time I ate anything substantial or even walked more than a few feet in my cell.

Now realizing how untrained I am and my lack of physical capability, it makes me want to get out even more. Once they take me back, I will have no way of getting out of whatever cell they put me in.

"Stop that and tell me your name, princess."

I stop moving, but I don't answer. I just stare at him.

Here is where he starts to get angry again, but there is no way for me to explain myself.

I don't speak.

I haven't talked since about a year or so after I got taken. Lashing out and asking them to stop made everything so much worse. One day, I just stopped, and I haven't said a single word since.

When he realizes I am not going to answer, he looks down at me and asks a little more forcefully

"WHAT IS YOUR NAME?"

"Alpha, I don't know if she speaks. She hasn't said a word since we got here," says the brunette.

"Dave, can you go back to the house and ask to borrow some of Hazel's clothes? We will be headed there right now."

So the brunette is Dave.

"Yes, Alpha," Dave says. He then starts running back into the woods away from us.

The big guy holding me looks down at me.

"Princess, can you please tell me your name?"

I look away shaking my head. I don't know him. I don't trust him. He could be as bad as the last people who abducted me, and I refuse to play into it.

I just look away, trying to find anything that will help me escape. When I realize that there is no way I can get away from the four fully grown men, any hope I had of getting away right now disappears.

When I look up, his eyes are full of sadness and sorrow. I try to focus on his expression, but I suddenly start getting very dizzy again. If this big man weren't carrying me, I would definitely be falling over by now.

I feel the man holding me start walking and then running, and right as I am about to pass out, I hear him yelling.

I try to look up to see where we are going, but everything goes blurry until it all fades to black.

Chapter 4

When I wake up, all I hear is the beeping of a machine and low sounds of voices from the hall.

"Is she up yet?" I recognize the voice as the big man who carried me from the woods.

"No, Alpha James. I gave her some sedatives a couple of hours back. She is still recovering. Even when she recovers from the wound on her leg, she isn't out of the woods yet. She is highly malnourished and has little to no muscle on her body. Wherever she was, she was not allowed out much, if ever. I am surprised she could shift at all. There is evidence she has been malnourished for years, and this is probably why she is so tiny," says the doctor. I also recognize him from the woods.

"Is there anything else wrong, Richard?"

"Aside from the obvious gash on her leg, she has minor cuts and bruises, but those will disappear in a couple of days. But there is something else you should know, and you have to be calm about this," says the doctor. I can hear the worry in his voice.

"What is it?"

"Wherever she was, it wasn't by her own will. The bruises on her ankles and wrists show signs of her being tied down or shackled, and with the number of scars she has, it is likely she was held for an extended period of time. Whatever trauma she has endured is probably causing her psychological issues."

"What did they do to her?" I hear the big guys voice boom.

"I'm not sure, but she has been through a lot. There is no medical reason for her silence; I believe she can speak but chooses not to. Also, I think she may be a teenager, but with her body so malnourished and her growth stunted, I couldn't really be sure about her exact age."

"I just don't understand what happened to her, and I want her to talk to me. I'm her mate. She should feel some type of pull by now. She must know what we mean for each other." I hear the big guy moving towards the room. I jump out of bed looking for a way, any way, out of this room.

When the guys at the cabin got angry, it was bad, and sometimes, I wasn't sure if they would kill me. There were a couple times I had come so close to death. I am not about to go through that again when I got a chance at freedom.

I look for a window or a door; there are no windows, but there is a second door.

When I stand up, I gasp at the pain in my leg. When I look down, I realize I was in one of those hospital gowns, and I could see the bottom half of my shin. There are stitches going up my leg, but it looks like it is healing rather quickly. The worst part is my thigh; I think it ripped open because I feel blood trickle down my leg.

I hear the door knob start to turn, and I panic. Not knowing what else to do, I run into the next room, only to find it is a bathroom. I jumped in the shower, hiding behind the curtain.

Now, I am not an idiot; I know he would find me.

But this gives me time to mentally prepare for whatever beating I am about to receive. I take deep breaths, in and out, while waiting. I hear him walk around the room, the sound of his footsteps getting closer.

The shower curtain flies back, and there stands the big guy, visibly angry and slightly panicked.

I cower away, hoping he will just leave although knowing that he won't. When he sees me crying while looking at him, he gets this confused look on his face.

"Why did you hide?"

His voice calms me down for a couple of seconds before someone else bursts through the bathroom door. When I look over, it's a girl who looks to be about twenty.

"What are you doing James?" she practically yells at him.

"I-I don't know, Hazel! I came to see how she was, and she ran," he says while frowning.

For some reason, it makes me upset to see him upset, but that makes no sense and just confuses me. I watch them both carefully while also looking around me. There is a window in the shower stall, but it's so small and so high that I don't think I could fit. Realizing they are between me and my only exit, I look back to Hazel and the big guy.

"Maybe it's because you came charging in here like a bull, James! She hasn't had the best couple of days, so maybe a huge guy running after her could have been what scared her?" She rolls her eyes and looks at me. "Hi, I'm Hazel. Don't worry, I'm not going to hurt you, and neither will he," she said, pointing at the James guy. James lets out a small growl that I whimper and curl into a ball again

"James, stop that! You are scaring her again!" she yells at him.

It's kind of a funny sight seeing this huge guy being yelled at by such a small girl. Hazel is only a couple inches taller than me, with blonde hair and, of course, hazel eyes.

When I look back at James, he looks sad again, realizing what happened.

"Go find Dave. You guys can do some work. I will get her cleaned up, and we will talk for a bit," Hazel says.

As James walks out the door, I get a little sad watching him leave but remind myself that I shouldn't feel bad for him.

Chapter 5

Once James is out of the room, I look back to Hazel.

"Sorry about him, but he is just a little protective with you being his mate and all. He got really worried when you didn't wake up for a couple of days." She slowly walks towards me with her hands up.

I am very confused as to why she is helping me or talking to me. I just want to leave. I want to be free and be on my own with nobody around me. I could live in the woods and take care of myself.

Before I was taken, I lived with a pack. My parents were the Alphas, but I didn't learn everything. All I knew were the basic workings of the pack. Werewolves don't turn until they turn a teenager at age thirteen, and that's when training and learning about everything being a werewolf is explained. But seeing as how I didn't make it to that age before being taken, I didn't learn much.

When she sees my confused look, she gets a little confused herself.

"Do you know a lot about werewolves?" she asks

I shrug.

"We're you in a pack before?"

I nod.

"Did you go rogue?"

I shake my head.

"Did you leave?" she asks, confused.

I shrug because I don't really know. I mean, they took me, so I was gone, but it wasn't my decision.

"Did you leave with your family?" she asks.

I shake my head again and look down. I can feel the tears gathering in my eyes, and I look down and play with my hands.

"Were you taken by strangers?"

I nod.

"For how long?"

I hold up nine fingers, then ten and shrug. I am not completely sure how long it has been.

"Ten weeks?" She looks sad.

I shake my head.

"Ten years?" Her eyes are now watering.

I nod.

She sniffles and looks away before looking back down and squatting to my level on the bathtub floor.

"James told me you haven't said much. Can you talk?"

I shrug and look away.

"Okay. That's fine. Maybe we can talk another time if you want to."

I nod. Before I realize what she is doing and attempt to stop her, she hugs me. But I don't mind, she isn't hurting me yet, so that must be a good sign.

***

After she hugged me and asked a couple yes or no questions about my leg and how much it hurt, she helped me wash it and called the doctor in to stitch it back up.

The doctor was nice to me and explained everything he was doing before he did it. My leg had to be numbed, and the shots hurt. When he started stitching it, I had to look away because it was not the most appealing thing to watch. After he leaves, Hazel stays to hang out with me for a little or to watch me. I'm not really sure which.

We hang out, and she talks about random things going on in the pack. She talks for a really long time. I don't know if she is trying to fill the silence, or if she is waiting for my input, but I just stare at her and think about how I am going to get away from here.

After an endless amount of time, but what was probably twenty minutes, she leaves to go get food, and my first opportunity to be alone and possibly escape arrives. I wait about a minute after she leaves then get up test the door.

To my surprise, it is unlocked. I open it slowly to peek out into the hallway. I slowly walk out and look to both sides before going to the right. I walk as fast as I can. This hallway opens up to a bigger hallway with a desk. Nobody is at the desk, and I look to the right to see two double doors leading to the outside.

I am a little skeptical about how easy this was, but I don't waste time to question it.

I quickly walk to the doors and open them. Outside, the sun is shining really bright, and I hold my hands above my eyes to block the sun while looking around. Straight ahead is a field. At the end of the field is dense forest. If I can get to the forest, I can escape and get away. They could chase after me, but I will hopefully have a substantial lead by the time Hazel gets back to the room and finds James or the doctor for help.

I start quickly walking across the field. I see people around, but no one is paying particular attention to me. I am almost in the woods when I hear someone yelling; I think they are yelling for me, so I start to go faster.

I am close to the woods when I feel big arms wrap around me and lift me off the ground. I start thrashing around and trying to get away. I need to get away.

"Calm down. I'm not going to hurt you."

Instantly I feel calm and recognize the voice as James', which makes me more nervous. I am still panicking, but I realize I will not be able to get away now. I start silently crying. He turns around and starts walking back to the building. As we get close, I see Hazel standing in the doorway. She looks worried and is standing there with her arms crossed.

As we get, closer James puts me down. I just keep my head down and wait for one of them to speak. I can feel James behind me, and he just sighs before turning around and walking away.

Hazel just stares at me with a sad look on her face.

"Let's go back inside; it's going to get dark soon." She turns around and walks inside, expecting me to follow her.

I turn around away from the building, but I see James halfway to a nearby house looking at me with his hands in his pockets. I turn around and quickly walk into the building, following Hazel. She is less scary than James, and I can try and get away later.

We make it back in the room, and she sits in a chair near the window and stares out the window.

"I don't know what you are scared of, and I don't know what happened, but nobody will harm you here. Nobody will ever lay a hand on you again, and I guess until you realize that, you are going to try to escape. I understand why you would want to, and I might do the same if I were you. I only ask that you wait until you are healed to do it. You aren't strong enough right now, and you will injure yourself more if you keep trying." She never looked at me. She seems sincere, but I don't know how I could trust strangers to be nice to me.

We sit there for a couple of minutes in complete silence. I walk from the doorway to the bed and sit down cross-legged. I start playing with my hands in my lap, and she picks up a sandwich off the table next to me and gives it to me. I give her a small smile, pick it up, and take a bite. She has one too, and we eat in silence for a little while.

After she eats, she sits there playing with some square device that lights up and shows pictures. She sees me looking at it and tells me it's an iPhone and explains what it does. I remember what a cell phone is, but they were just phones you could flip open and call people.

Hazel gives me some shorts and a long sleeve shirt I can change into, and I head into the bathroom and change quickly. Afterward, she explains they want me to stay here overnight, but I can leave the hospital tomorrow. When she says I can leave, I get excited before she corrects herself and says only the hospital.

When she sees my face fall, she looks disappointed and sighs before asking me if I'm tired. I shrug and sit back on the bed.

She then asks if I want to watch a movie, so I nod my head, and we begin watching a movie called *The Notebook*.

In the end, I am tearing up a little, and I look over to see she is too. Realizing how late it is, she says she has to start heading back home but promises to be back tomorrow morning.

She says that someone will be outside the hospital, and there are overnight doctors and nurses that will help me.

She is probably just telling me this so I know to not try to run again.

Chapter 6

The next morning, I wake up to seeing Hazel with a little girl coloring on a small table next to my bed. I sit up, and the little girl looks up at me. She is a carbon copy of Hazel. She has the blonde hair with those same piercing hazel eyes.

She runs up to me when she sees me awake.

"Hi, I'm Callie, and mommy said we could come color with you this morning." She has that slightly childish twist on her words, and I would guess that she is 4 or 5. I just smile in response.

"Wanna color?" she asks. I look up at Hazel to see her smiling at us, sitting in a chair next to the table. I just nod my head, and Callie brings up a couple of her coloring books and sits on the foot of my bed, crisscrossing her legs and handing me a princess notebook.

We start coloring in silence until Callie looks up at me again. "What's your name?"

Not knowing what to do, I just stare at her then look at Hazel who quickly tells Callie to color and mind her business.

I feel bad, but I realize I haven't told anybody my name yet, not that I could have anyway. Looking at Callie, I write it down above the princess I am coloring. My handwriting is barely legible, and I haven't written in years, so I am surprised I even remember.

Fifteen minutes later, I am completely done coloring the princess. I hand Callie the notebook back. She looks at the page before noticing my writing at the top. She looks at Hazel still on the floor.

"Mommy, what does this say? She wrote me a note with the princess!" Hazel quickly walks over confused until she looks at the name on the top.

"Grace," Hazel says.

"The princess's name is Grace? That's not right. This is supposed to be Cinderella, Mommy!" Callie says, clearly distraught and confused.

"No, honey, she is telling you that her name is Grace."

Callie makes an 'o' with her mouth and looks at me. "I think that's a really pretty name!" she says, jumping and hugging me. I just smile and hug her back.

"I think it's a really pretty name too," says a deep voice from the doorway. I look up to see James just standing there, leaning against the doorway.

When I look at him, I am not as scared as I was yesterday. I realize that he is really good looking, and with his calm expression, he doesn't really look all that scary anymore. When I realize I am checking him out, and everybody is staring at me, I quickly blush and look down.

Luckily, he starts speaking without acknowledging the fact that I blatantly stared and checked him out.

"The doctor says you are good to leave, but you will need to come back in a couple of days so he can look at your leg. He has a new diet for you to help you gain some weight and help your muscles build back up. He also said you can't do any strenuous activity because even walking and running is going to be difficult for you until your muscles come back normally." Throughout his entire speech, I just continue to stare at him. I am at a loss for what to do because I am clearly not good at holding a conversation and the guys at the cabin never really talked to me anyways. I just nod my head.

I am again blatantly staring at James, but I can't help it, he is very attractive. If this were another life, I would definitely want to be around him and be with him.

"Grace?" I hear my name being called. I look up to see Hazel looking at me worriedly. I nod, and then James starts speaking again.

"I can help you get back to the house or if you want, Hazel can bring you there and hang out with you," he says while looking around the room, trying not to seem upset when he says Hazel can hang out with me.

I slowly stand up and get my balance on my wobbly legs before walking over to him at the door. When I got closer, I notice him visibly tense up before I reach my hand out and touch his face. When he picked me up the very first time we met, I felt tingles across my skin, and it was somewhat alarming.

This time, when my fingers make contact, tingles shoot up my arm, causing me to jump back and almost fall before two arms wrap around my waist with those same tingles going through me. I look up and see James has caught me, and when I am back on my feet, he lets me go.

To be honest, the sensation was not painful. They actually felt nice.

Hazel clears her throat behind us, and I turn around. I completely forgot her and Callie are in the room.

"Well, I have to get Callie back for her nap soon... but if you want me to stay, I can, Grace," Hazel says. I just shake my head.

She and Callie gather all of their things before leaving. When they walk by, Callie hugs onto my leg tight and whispers, "I hope you will play with me again sometime," before following her mother and running out of the room.

I smile watching her go, and when I look up at James, he is looking at me with the look of pure happiness, like a child on Christmas.

Chapter 7

After minutes of awkward silence, James asks me if I want to walk back to the house, seeing as it is less than a half a mile away from this house. I nod, and we begin our walk out of the building.

We walk out of the house and into the sunlight, and it takes a couple of minutes to adjust to the brightness. I look around and notice that it is reasonably warm with a slight breeze. I am only wearing cotton shorts and a long sleeve shirt, though; I shiver a bit and cross my arms, hugging myself.

I feel someone's gaze on me, and I look over to see James looking at me worriedly. He looks torn like he doesn't know if he should help or keep his distance. After looking at him a bit more, I make the decision for him and start walking closer to him with our arms barely brushing against each other. His skin feels unusually warm, and I try and brush up against him to feel the warmth.

If I am going to try to run away later, maybe being nice and making it seem like I am not trying to escape will make them trust me.

I look up at him, and the smile he gives me has to be the most breathtaking smile I have ever seen. It lights up his whole face, and you can just feel the happiness radiating off him. I don't know why this small gesture would make him happy, and that's when I remember what Hazel said about mates.

I will have to figure out about that later.

***

About a half an hour later, we arrive at a house which is easily the size of a mansion. We took a little longer because of how slow I walk. I am very out of breath and slow because I hadn't walked very far when I was a captive. I had a little 5-by-5 cell, and I was never allowed to leave, except when they had chores and things for me to do. The two times I did try to escape, I never made it far, and I was brutally punished for both times.

We make our way into the house, and once inside, I look at how nice the place is. It has wooden floors with a chandelier right in the front entrance.

"Would you like anything to drink or eat? Or we could take a tour of the house? If you are tired, you can rest too if that's what you want. Or I could call Hazel if you would rather be with her. I understand. It's fine. I'll go call Hazel." He looks visibly nervous as he rambles and starts walking away, but I grab his arm before he gets more than a foot away and stop him. I shake my head no, and he looks slightly confused.

Not really knowing how to communicate, I point to my mouth and shrug.

"Hungry?" he asks a little hesitantly. I nod and give him a small smile.

"Okay, well, I have plenty of food. I mean, I'm not a good cook, but we can figure something out," he says with some enthusiasm.

We make it to the kitchen a couple of minutes later, and I look around at how big and extravagant everything in this house is. There are stainless steel appliances everywhere with marble countertop and a huge double door refrigerator. When we get there, he pulls out a stool for me and turns to walk towards the refrigerator.

"What would you like? We have some pizza, some pasta, fruits. Are you thirsty?" He turns around and looks at me, and I nod.

"Water or juice?" he asks me. I hold up my first finger hoping he gets what I mean.

"Water?" he asks, and I nod my head. I smile, knowing there is some way to communicate with him.

He pours me a glass of water then gives me three more options.

"Pizza, pasta, or fruit?" he asks as I gulp down my water.

I hold up three fingers.

"Fruit it is! Apples, grapes, watermelon or we could make a fruit salad?" he asks, looking at me. I think for a minute then hold up four fingers.

Seeing my answer, he reaches in and grabs all of the fruit and carries it to the countertop in front of me. He puts it all in a big bowl and gets us two forks. We start eating, and while we do, he starts talking about himself; how he has a younger sister, but she lives in another pack with her mate; his favorite color is green; he hates lasagna, and spring is his favorite season.

In my opinion, he is just filling the silence because of my lack of input, but oddly, it is comforting to just listen to his voice even when he talks about silly things like the seasons.

I find myself smiling, looking up at him when he starts telling me about his friends and Hazel.

Hazel is married to Dave, the brunette from the woods. Callie is their daughter, and she is four. Dave is his second in command and helps James run the pack when James needs it or is out of town. Technically, Dave's title is beta, but they have been best friends since they were toddlers and they rarely call each other by their titles. I learned that Hazel is, in fact, a couple of years older than me at twenty-one. And Dave is twenty-two. The third guy from the woods is Cole who is the third in command and helps when the alpha and beta aren't around. His main job is guarding the Luna when she is found and becomes a part of the pack. James starts talking about how that will be me, and Cole will be my guard. That confused me until I remember that James is the alpha of this pack. My eyes go wide, and I start to panic.

When James looks over at me, he gets confused. "What's wrong, Grace?" he asks.

I just shake my head back and forth while tears threaten to come out. They are going to have someone watching me at all times. Any chance of ever going off to live my own life is now gone.

I start to panic and struggle to breathe. James puts his arms around me and pulls me onto his lap, rubbing my back, and trying to get me to calm down.

Minutes later, I feel a little calmer. Being in James' arms is very comforting, and I still don't understand why or why he even has me here.

I lift my head up and look into his eyes, realizing that they are bright green just like mine. When I reach up to touch his face, I feel those same tingles again and realize I am feeling them everywhere on my body that has made contact with his body. Confused, I look down at my hand, pulling it away from his face.

"It's the mate bond," he says softly. I look up at him confused as a realization dawns in his eyes. "You don't know what that is, do you?" he asks.

I shake my head, and he starts to explain.

"A mate for wolves, like me and you, is like your soul mate, your other half. They complete you in a way that nobody else can, and the two are meant to be together. It is not instantaneous, but eventually, they will know everything about you and understand your needs and wants, your hopes and dreams. They will understand you better than anyone else ever could. Humans have soul mates too, but they can't tell when they finally meet them like we do, and more often than not, they don't end up with them.

"Werewolves have certain signs when they meet their soul mate. For example, the tingles you feel. You won't feel it with anyone else but your mate. I don't know about you, but for me, they are very comforting, and it lets me know you are right next to me and safe. Another is your wolf telling you that that person is your mate. They are the main reason we know when we have found our mates. They recognize each other because our human halves can't. Every wolf only has one mate, and a few are unlucky enough not to find theirs. People usually find their mates by the age of eighteen. I had almost completely given up on finding you." Towards the end of his speech, he looks down, but not before I see a sad look in his eyes.

I suddenly feel bad.

"Grace, I don't know what happened to you, but I would like to..."
He trails off.

Shaking my head, I try and get up, looking for an escape route. I can't do this.

When he realizes this, he holds me tighter and starts shushing me, trying to get me to calm down.

"Grace, calm down. Nobody is going to lay a finger on you."

I look up at him to see a look on his face I have never seen before. He looks determined, even protective.

"Grace, nobody will ever hurt you. I will make sure of that. Please trust me. You are the most important person in my life, and I will never let anyone else hurt you again. You don't have to tell me what happened now, but someday soon I think you should let somebody know. It can't be easy what you went through." He looks visibly upset and distraught.

I don't like to see him upset, and I don't know what to do to help him. I bring my hands up to his face and tilt his head up, wiping at the one tear that escaped. He smiles and brings his head closer to mine, looking down at my lips. Right before we are about to kiss, he pulls back and looks at me in the eye. He grabs my face and lightly kisses my forehead. I close my eyes and take a deep breath before opening them and looking at him.

Seconds later, I lean in and kiss him lightly on the lips. If touching him and feeling those tingles were nice, it was nothing compared to kissing him. It's like fireworks going on in my head, and my chest feels all warm and fluttery. A few seconds later, he pulls back and looks at me with a smile on his face. He hugs me and buries his head in my neck, breathing slowly.

When I look out the window, I realize we have been eating and talking for hours, and it's now dark out. I look at the clock and see it is about nine at night.

"Want to go to bed?" James asks. I blush and look down, nodding my head. He lifts my head up and kisses my red cheeks, "Alright, let's go then."

When he stands up, he doesn't put me down. Instead, he carries me towards the stairs. Enjoying the feeling, I lay my head on his shoulder while I have my arms wrapped around his neck and my legs around his waist.

Seeing as he is almost double my size and height, he has no problem carrying me up the stairs and into a room.

Chapter 8

When we get into the room, the first thing I notice is the scent. This is definitely James' room. I look around the room, and I see a bunch of picture frames on shelves that have books. The walls are a light gray, and the bed has a navy blue comforter with red sheets. The bed is absolutely massive. It has to be the biggest bed I have ever seen and has these huge fluffy pillows on top of them.

James puts me down and watches me as I look around his room, checking all of his pictures and books. There is also a desk in the far corner and a couch against one of the longer walls. When I turn around to look at him, he is still standing in the doorway looking slightly nervous.

"This is my room, and you will be sleeping in here with me."

My eyes widen at this statement. I nervously look over at the bed.

"I can sleep on the couch for a couple of nights if you want. I really don't mind it." He trails off. When he looks back at me, I just nod, too nervous to do anything else.

"Do you want to shower?" I feel my face get red at him mentioning the shower, and I get nervous. "You can shower alone. The doctor says you will tire easily because of how little muscle you have, so you need to let me know if you need help. I'll go start it for you," he says this all in a rush while walking to the bathroom.

He walks back out and into his closet and comes out with one of his shirts and basketball shorts. "You can wear this to bed if you want. I don't have any clothes for you, but maybe you can go shopping later in the week with Hazel?"

I nod my head, take the clothes, and head into the bathroom.

After trying to wash my hair and dirt around my body, I am relatively clean, and I walk out and look at myself in the mirror.

I realize I missed about half the dirt on my back and neck and my hair still has conditioner in it. Realizing how exhausted I was after ten minutes by myself, I know I won't be able to do the rest myself. I walk out of the bathroom, still in the towel and look at James sitting on the bed.

He looks up at me, and I point to my back, neck, and hair and frown.

"Need help?" he asks with a small smile. I nod my head and walk back in knowing he will follow.

He walks in and starts the water again but makes a bath this time instead. He puts bubbles in it, and when it is filled up, he turns around while I get in and sit down. He pulls down the shower head and helps me wash out the rest of my hair.

When he is done with my hair, he gets the body wash and starts washing my back. When I see the bubbles in the water, I get a funny idea. Gathering a handful of suds, I turn around and blow them on James.

At first, he looks shocked, and for a second I get scared thinking he is going to get mad, but then a second later, he scoops bubbles with his hands and put them on my head. I splash him and start laughing. When I laugh, he freezes, and I turn back around to look at him.

He is smiling, so big it stretches across his entire face. "Your laugh is beautiful," he says with a grin.

I look down, and I can feel myself getting red. He lifts up my chin and looks directly into my eyes.

"Don't be embarrassed. I love it." He smiles. When he leans in close enough to kiss me, I grab his shirt and pull him into the tub, splashing water over the side of the tub and on to the floor. I start laughing again and look down at a very soaked James sitting next to me. He smiles mischievously and starts tickling me, causing me to laugh even louder.

Now you would think having this huge man in a tub isn't possible with me in it too, but everything in this house is huge. It's bigger than a mansion, and I don't even know what I could compare it to; it comes close to the size of a hotel but with not as many floors. The bath tub is easily the size of a jacuzzi, so we fit pretty easily.

After a couple of minutes, he stops and just wraps his arms around me, holding me against his chest while I sit in his lap. Even though I am on his lap, I still have to look up at him. I curl in a ball and just rest my head on his chest feeling relaxed and for once in my life, safe.

***

After twenty minutes or so, we get out, and James goes to get changed. I wear the shirt and shorts he gave me. The shirt is like a dress that goes right above my knees, and the shorts don't fit, so I just leave those off. When I walk out, James has changed and is just wearing shorts. His back is facing towards me, doing something with the TV while I just stare at him from behind. He is about 6'4" with muscles on muscles. His dark hair has that scruffy look to it, and he has a nice tan to his body.

He turns around, and I realize I am staring at him. I quickly run and go to sit on the bed. The bed is very soft, and I already feel myself getting comfortable. At the cabin, I used to sleep on the floor with a blanket and pillow.

"Would you like to watch TV or anything?" James asks.

I just yawn and shrug my shoulders.

"We can just go to bed then," he says while shutting off the TV. When he goes to switch off the light, and there is darkness, I start to panic. I have no idea where in the room he is.

What if he decides he doesn't want to sleep on the couch? He will try sleeping with me!

"Grace, calm down. I can hear your heartbeat from here. Do you want me to turn on the bathroom light?" About two seconds later the bathroom, to the left of the bed, illuminates the rest of the room. He is looking at me with concern written all over his face.

He shuts the door until it is open by a crack, and then I see him walk over to the couch and lie down.

"Goodnight, Grace."

***

I could feel their hands all over me as I am tied down, thrashing around. They won't be done anytime soon; this is how they always start it.

"Come on, Gracie, you deserve this. Gracie, you know you like this. The big bad alpha's daughter begging for mercy," I hear Kyle, the worst of the rouges, saying.

I refuse to say anything, knowing that it will do me no good.

"Better yet, beg me to stop and I will, Gracie. You just gotta say the word, darling."

Lie. They never stop.

I can hear my heart pounding in my ears as they take the rags of clothes I have off my body. I silently start to cry while they start undressing me.

"Gracie, be still," another one yells.

I thrash around, and seconds later, I feel a sharp stinging on my cheek as my head turns to the side. Another slap, not too hard this time.

They all keep shouting my name, taunting to get me to speak.

"Grace! Grace!"

Suddenly, I awake to a large man standing over me, shaking my shoulders. I realize I am all sweaty and my eyes are already wet from crying. I am tangled in sheets in a huge bed, and as I realize I don't have a bed, I start to panic. Seeing the man walking over to sit next to me, I scramble to get away and end up falling off the other side of the bed near a window.

"Grace? Grace, talk to me. What's wrong?" he asks as he approaches me. I pull my knees up and wrap my arms around them, putting my head down, silently begging him not to come over. I can't take another beating tonight.

Why don't they ever give me a break? My whole body is shaking in anticipation.

When I don't hear anything a minute later, I look up and see the man standing in front of me. What surprises me is the look of absolute horror that is written all over his face. He must be new because I don't remember any of the men looking this good. He looks somewhat familiar, now that I think about it.

"Grace, don't you remember me? It's me... James," he says.

As I continued to stare at him, all of the memories of the past two days come crashing down on me like a ton of bricks. I finally realize that I just had a dream. A couple seconds later, I hear a shuffling and look up to see him walking over back to me. No!

I hold my hand up again and try to scoot farther back until my back is already against the wall.

"Grace, you remember now, don't you?" James asks, looking completely hurt. I just give him a nod. Just because he is nice to me now doesn't mean this is how it's going to be. I am still locked up in here with him.

At first, they were nice to me too.

Chapter 9

When I look up again, the man just sits on the ground across from me. Confused, I just stare blankly at him.

"I am not going to hurt you, Gracie, and I am—"

Hearing that nickname, I lose it and start crying again.

He is just *like them*.

I start breathing heavily, and before I know it, my throat feels like it's closing and I start to gasp for breath.

"Grace, what is it? Grace, princess, you have to breathe!" My vision starts to go blurry, and I start to see black dots everywhere.

"Grace, look at me!" A deep voice booms at me. I look over to where it is coming from and see James sitting under me now.

"Grace, look at me right now. Breathe in and out, look at me, watch me. Nothing is going to get you. You are safe." His voice is so comforting. I listen to him, trying to breathe in and out as he says.

A couple of minutes later, my breathing is back under control. His deep chocolate eyes are staring at me as I stare right back at him.

I scramble to get off of his lap. I scoot back until I realize my back is now against the bed.

"Grace?" he says.

He moves towards me, but I start panicking again and look for the door. It must be on the other side of this bed. I see the door to the bathroom and wonder if I can make it there before him.

Deciding I might as well give it a shot, I dash towards the bathroom and hear him mutter curses as he gets up to run after me. I get in, but before I can shut the door, he sticks his foot in the doorway and stops it just inches before it closes.

I try and push it closed until I realize James is the size of the Hulk. I move up and wait for him to come in. He slowly opens the door and stares at me, looking sad and upset. I stare back confused.

What is he doing? Why am I not being punished?

"Grace, I am not going to hurt you. I will take however long to prove that to you, but I am also not going to leave you alone while you are upset."

I just nod my head. I know he is lying, but a part of me wants to believe everything he is saying.

"Do you want to go get some breakfast? It's still early, about 5, I think, but I can make you something if you want." I just nod at him. Either I walk, or he drags me. I prefer the former.

He starts walking, looking back to make to sure I am following him. This continues all the way downstairs. After the first three flights of stairs, I quickly start to get tired and run out of breath. I sit on the steps, and about six steps later, he turns around and sees me sitting.

"Do you want help?" He starts walking back up, but I scoot back a couple of steps.

"Okay, okay we can take a break." He sits down about ten steps below me. "So do you want pancakes, eggs, or some cereal?" I shrug my shoulders. I haven't had eggs or cereal since before, but the guys always made me make them pancakes.

I actually enjoyed cooking because it was the only time I was off limits for them to hurt.

I stand up, and he asks if I am okay, and I just nod at him. We make it all the way downstairs and into the kitchen.

Why is everything in this house so dang big?

"I can make pancakes if you want. Those are easy," he says while walking around the kitchen.

I walk over to him as he turns on the skillet. He jumps as I touch his arm, and I jump back at his reaction. I quickly look down.

Shit! I shouldn't have done that.

I turn around to run, but he wraps his arms around my waist before I can.

"Grace, what's wrong? I'm not going to hurt you. Just look at me." I turn around in his arms and see him looking down at me with a confused look on his face. "What did you need, Grace?" he asks.

I grab his arms from around my waist and undo them, holding his hand. I look down at his massive hand engulfing mine. Before he can do anything, I tug him towards the counter where the seats are and sit him down in one.

I then walk over and begin getting all of the stuff for pancakes. I can feel his gaze on me the entire time as I prepared the ingredients.

A couple of seconds later, he begins to speak. "Grace, I can do that, you know. You don't have to." He begins to stand up, and I hold my hand up and shake my head no. He sits back down.

Ten minutes later, I have the pancakes done, but the kitchen a little messy. I put a stack of pancakes on a plate and give them to James while I begin to clean the kitchen.

"What are you doing?" he asks.

I stare back at the countertops confused. Cleaning?

"No, Grace, make yourself a plate and come eat." I grab one pancake and go two seats down from him. He scoots down so we are only one chair away and puts one of his pancakes on my plate.

"You are going to eat more, Grace. You need to. It's not good to eat so little."

I stare at my plate completely confused.

All of this for me? Is this a test? Am I actually allowed to eat this much?

I eat the first pancake and look over to see him munching away on his pancakes while looking at me.

"Princess, you better be starting on that second pancake."

Chapter 10

After I finally finish the second pancake, I get up to clear the plates away.

"Princess, sit down. I am capable of cleaning," James says. He takes the plates away and begins clearing the rest.

I get up to help, grabbing the mixing bowl and walking towards the sink. When he turns around from putting the plates in the sink, he starts to come towards me. When he sees the dirty bowl I am holding, he comes to try to grab it.

"Grace, what did I say? You don't have to—" I drop the bowl as his hands make contact with mine, causing the bowl to shatter on the floor at my feet and the excess batter to go everywhere.

I start to panic. Hurriedly, I bend down to grab the glass and walk around to get towels to wipe the batter off the floor before he gets mad.

I should really pay attention to what I'm doing. I am going to be in so much trouble for this.

"Grace, stop! Grace, you are walking on glass with bare feet."

I stop and look down at my feet, waiting for him to hit me. Looking down at the mess I created, I realize my feet are already bleeding from the fresh cuts. I frown at the blood splatter on the floor. Another mess to clean up.

A couple of seconds later, I feel him pick me up and sit me on the counter. "Just stay there, Grace. Please." I look up. He looks upset.

Why couldn't I just stay sitting as he wanted me to? I wouldn't have broken the bowl, and I wouldn't be in trouble right now if I just did what he had told me to do. I start crying, waiting to get into trouble.

Once he is all done cleaning the floor, he starts walking over to me with a wash cloth and a first aid kit. I scoot back on the counter, suddenly nervous.

"Hey, hey, hey, Grace, calm down. Everything is okay. You are going to be okay. I just have to clean your feet and see if there are any shards in the cuts." He bends down and starts wiping my feet, but they just keep bleeding.

I think I feel a chip on my left foot. It is perfect to go with the gash along my thigh.

"Well, this one might need stitches, and I don't know if I can get the glass out. We are going to have to walk back to the doctors." He looks at me nervously. "Is it okay if I carry you? You can't walk with splinters of the glass bowl in your foot."

I just nod in agreement.

***

About an hour later, the doctor is done stitching up my foot. Turns out that splinter that was able to cut deep was about a half an inch long. They were shocked that I couldn't feel it. I guess I panicked more at the mess I made than at the situation of my feet.

"Okay now, Grace, you won't be able to walk on that foot for a while. If you do, the stitches will rip and you will be right back here, okay? Try to stay off that leg. The cut is pretty deep," Dr. Richard says. I just nod my head. "I can give you crutches if you would like, but those may be hard for you to use, and it may be better just to rest or have someone carry you."

I look over at James to see him smirking a little bit, and my cheeks start to heat up. Why am I embarrassed? I should be scared, but weirdly enough, I'm not as scared as I was earlier. Also, why is James so excited about carrying me around all the time?

"Thanks, Richard," James says. He comes over to me, and I don't back away when he picks me up.

We start heading back to the house, and I realize that this is easily a ten-minute walk that only took so long the other day because of my slow pace. When we get back to the house, he brings me up to his room and sits me down on the bed.

"Princess, I know you were trying to help, but you really don't have to do a lot, okay? I need you resting and eating plenty so you can get better. It's only about 8 right now, so I was wondering if you would want to spend the day together. I mean, if you want to…" He looks down shyly.

We are gonna spend the whole day together, Gracie.

That was the first time. I was eight. Only a month after I was being taken. They never even thought about what they were doing to a little girl because they didn't have a care in the world. Rogues are rogues for a reason: they care about no one but themselves.

I won't even get a month with James before he starts doing the same things they did to me.

For what feels like the thousandth time since I have met James and being taken back here, I feel myself begin to panic as I mentally prepare for I know what will come.

Chapter 11

"Grace? What's wrong?" James is looking at me.

I don't say anything. I mean, if he is going to touch me like they did, he might as well just do it. It was the perfect timing too because now I am injured, and I can't fight back.

What I never seem to understand is why I cry every time. You would think it would get easier, less hurtful somehow. But every time, it kills me a little more on the inside.

I just close my eyes with tears running down my face and wait. After a couple of seconds, I feel something on my cheek. I look up and see him staring down at me, wiping my tears away with his thumb as a profound sadness makes its way to his eyes.

"Princess, I don't know what's going on in that head of yours, and trust me I wish I did, but whatever it is, I hope you know I would never hurt you. You are my life now, princess, and I want to make you happy." He now has tears in his eyes. "I just don't know how," he mumbles the last part, but I still hear it anyways.

"I'll be downstairs finishing the dishes and cleaning. Maybe when I get back up, we can watch a movie or something?" He hesitates before getting up. "I know you are still scared and hurt, and I don't know who did it or why, but we need to talk sometime soon. If that means you writing it down or me guessing, I don't care, but there are some things you have to tell me." With that, he gets up and walks out of the room.

Minutes later, I am falling asleep with his smell surrounding me and the picture of his smile from yesterday in my mind.

***

Something really hot is surrounding me. I can feel myself burning up.

I open my eyes to see a shirt in front of me while I am on my side, and somebody very warm is wearing this shirt. I try to scoot back and realize there is an arm around the back of my body. When I look around, I see that I am curled in a ball next to James with his arm around my torso, keeping me in a cocoon under his arm.

Well, I guess I'm pretty small, and he is close to the Incredible Hulk.

I look towards the window and see the sun start to go down, making it around late afternoon. I look at James' face and see his eyes are closed. The way our bodies are positioned feels safe, like he is protecting anything from getting to me. While I watch him sleep, I realize he isn't all that scary when he is relaxed.

I uncurl my arm from around my legs and reach out to touch the shirt on his side. I press my small palm into his side, and he stirs underneath me. When I look back up, he is staring directly at me, and I get lost in his eyes.

Moments like this are what confuse me. Men are scary. Men do bad things, but James isn't scary. James isn't mean. And James doesn't do bad things.

That I know about.

Everything in me is telling me to trust him, but I can't just yet.

"Princess, we need to talk." Tears come to my eyes, and I shake my head no while burying myself back into his side. "If you don't want to talk to me, that's fine, I understand, but sooner or later you are going to have to talk to someone about what happened. All I know right now is that I found you in the woods near death, you are very underweight and unhealthy, and you look like you have been through a lot for someone your age. I mean I don't even know how old you are. All I know is that your name is Grace."

When I look up into his eyes, I realize his eyes are turning black again. I reach out and touch his side, and they start to dim back to brown. He looks down at me, and I hold up one finger, then eight. I should be eighteen and turn nineteen soon. It is almost fall, and this will be the tenth fall since I went missing right before my ninth birthday.

He nods his head, gives me a small smile, then looks up and stares at the ceiling.

***

We spend the rest of the day in his bed lying down, watching movies. He brought up a couple of sandwiches and chips for dinner. The night passes smoothly, but as soon as it is time to go back to sleep, I get nervous. Aside from waking up under his arm, we haven't been physically close all day. Will he want to cuddle again?

Do I want to cuddle again?

"Princess, do you want to go to bed now? It's nearly midnight." He looks over at me. We are both sitting down on the bed after just finishing another movie called *Titanic*. That was a really sad movie.

I just nod my head.

"Do you want to shower again? You will have to take the bath so you aren't standing, and I'm not sure if you can get those stitches on your feet wet." I just nod my head, and he picks me up and brings me to the bathroom. He sets me on the counter, runs the bath and sits me on the edge of the tub.

"I'll be back in about ten minutes, okay? I'll be right outside the door if you need me, just knock on the wall." He walks out, and I slowly go through the slow process of taking his t-shirt off and getting in the tub.

Ten minutes later, I try to lift myself out of the tub and reach for the towel hanging off to the side. Once I am finally out, I wrap the towel around myself and lay on the floor exhausted. A couple of seconds later, I hear a knock on the door, and James walks in. When he looks down at me, he looks concerned.

"Grace? Are you okay? Did you fall?" He comes over to try and lift me up, but I just hold out my hand for him to stop. I really don't feel like moving again.

"You didn't fall?"

I shake my head and close my eyes again.

"I had Hazel drop off some clothes earlier today while you were sleeping. You can put on some PJ's when you are ready."

I just nod my head and keep my eyes closed for another minute.

I sit up and look around for the clothes to see them in James' hand. I hold out my hand, and he gives them to me. I give him a small smile and then look towards the door. His face is getting a light shade of pink to it.

"Right, well… I'll be out there, just knock on the door once you are done."

After a slight struggle, I put on the light pink shorts and white long sleeve shirt. I feel the material. It's not rough like the clothes I used to have, but rather very soft. I knock on the door, and James comes in and lifts me up and puts me on the bed.

"Okay, goodnight, Grace." He moves to walk away, and I instantly grab his arm. He looks down at me, and I look at the bed. Realizing what I just asked, my face gets red, and I let go of his arm. "Do you want me to sleep with you? I won't touch you. I can stay on my side if you want." I can practically hear his smile while he is talking.

I just shrug while scooting over to the other side, and he lowers himself down, turning off the light on the nightstand.

"Goodnight, princess."

After a few minutes of rolling around and occasionally looking over at James, I see him with his eyes closed. I then move another couple of inches closer to him. As if he can see me, he moves his arm out, so there is enough space for me to curl up next to him if I want to.

After a few minutes of deliberation, I move over and curl myself under his arm, holding onto the side of his shirt with my hand. His arm moves closer and presses into my back, and in minutes, I am sleeping soundly.

***

The rest of the week passes with us hanging out in his room and watching movies and him telling me things about his pack and his family. His parents, William and Isabelle, are both alive and very happy. They live in their own house away from the pack house now that James is the alpha.

We have been in the pack house the entire week, but since we are on the sixth floor and the entire floor is the alpha's, I haven't seen any of the pack. The day we went down for breakfast, everybody was still asleep, and I haven't stepped out of the room since.

James has explained a lot to me, and it is interesting knowing everything about werewolves. The one I had no idea about as a child was the mind link. It is a pack link that connects everyone in the pack. Werewolves can mind link with certain members or groups of the pack, and the alphas can send mind links to everyone all at once. It's basically like reading each other's minds and being able to talk to each other without actually having to talk. I don't hear anyone because, technically, I don't belong to a pack anymore and werewolves only get the mind link after they shift.

I am now more comfortable around James, but there is no way I want to meet the pack yet. James explained more in detail about mates and marking and all of that. Marking is when the male bites on a certain part of the female's shoulder with their canines and a tattoo-like mark will appear within twenty-four hours. Females can mark the males too, but until recent years, it wasn't very common. It was very embarrassing that I got confused when he talked about completing the mating process.

Basically, it was a talk about the birds and the bees and, considering I have never had that talk before, it was embarrassing. I know how it all works, but James had to explain that that's how we would be like; we would be officially mated for life and that would make me a part of his pack and I would be able to mind link with them. Once the mating and marking happen, werewolves are mated for life, and they can feel each other's emotions and know when another is hurt or in trouble. The only way to break the bond is if one person dies, which James assured me was not going to happen until we were ninety and wrinkly.

I'm not ready for the marking or mating, and James said we don't have to, but whenever I am ready or if I want to, we can. He did say he would have to mark me before I meet the pack. Apparently, they don't have to happen at the same time, which means he can mark me and our minds will start to mind link and everything, but we won't have to mate. It just lets everyone know whose mate I am and what my rank is. That scares me because he says it will hurt for a couple of seconds, but he also said if he marks me, the pack will know I am his mate, and they will never try to hurt me. Right now it is Friday, and James says he has to go help with the pack since he has been gone all week. He called Hazel, and she should be coming over with Callie soon to hang out for the day. We are having a 'girl's day, ' but I don't know what Hazel's idea of a girl's day includes. I can't even walk still.

"Gracieeeeeee!" yells Callie, running into the room. At the mention of that name, my throat starts to close, and I start breathing heavily. Why does everybody need to call me that? Within seconds, I am on James' lap, and he is trying to get me to look at him

"Grace, look at me. Breathe, Princess… Everything is going to be okay. You are fine. Everything is fine. Nobody is going to hurt you."

As I listen to his voice, I slowly calm down, and my breathing is back to normal. I look up and give him a small smile before I look over to see Callie in Hazel's arms looking very upset.

"Grace, what's wrong? Why are you crying?" Callie asks.

I just smile back at her and bury my head in James' chest, breathing in his scent.

"Callie, please don't call Grace Gracie anymore. She doesn't like that nickname, and it makes her upset. Okay?" James gently but firmly, says.

"Okay! Can I call her something else then? Like my own special nickname?"

"Sure. As long as Grace is okay with it." James looks down at me, and I just nod my head.

"Can I call you Cece?" Callie asks.

I nod my head and smile.

Cece. I have never been called that before.

"Okay. Well, I need to head down, see Dave and start on some work. If you need me, I'll either be on the ground floor in my office or out on patrol with some of the guys. If you need me, just have Hazel contact me, okay?" I nod my head, and he gets up while placing me back on the bed, kissing my forehead, and walking out the door.

"Okay so, who's ready to paint some nails?"

Chapter 12

The whole day passes rather quickly. We painted our nails and toenails in the morning. I painted Callie's, and she got very excited when I put a red heart on her big toe. Callie painted Hazel's, which Hazel repainted after, and Hazel painted mine.

We had lunch, and a nice girl named Brittany brought up our food.

After lunch, Hazel asks if I wanted to get a haircut. My hair is down past my waist and extremely hard to deal with, so I agree.

"Okay, so I am having Cassidy come here so it's easier and we don't have to go all the way across town. She should be here in about fifteen minutes, and it will only take about a half an hour or so."

I just nod and look over at Callie who is now passed out on the couch.

"So how have you been? James has been nice, right?" Hazel asks.

I laugh a little and nod my head

"Good. I wouldn't want to have to kick his butt."

I laugh again.

"Did he explain to you everything about mates and packs and alphas and everything?" I nod my head again.

"Good. Well, if you have any questions, you can always ask me."

I nod again and smile at her. I think we will be good friends.

***

An hour or so later, my hair is cut, Cassidy is leaving, and Hazel is helping me blow dry and straighten my hair. I got it cut up to about 4 or 5 inches below my shoulder. Cassidy said this would make it easier since I don't really know what to do with it.

Right now, Hazel is in the bathroom with me while I sit on a chair. She is teaching me how to use the blow dryer and the hair straightener. She says we can curl my hair if I want, too. My natural waves look good anyways, she says, so I don't need to do anything to it really, but she wants to show me so I can do it whenever I like. She then promises to buy me the right hair stuff I need when we go shopping.

After my hair is straightened and slightly waved at the end, Hazel brings me some more clothes, telling me how she bought me undergarments since I ran out about mid-week. I change into the leggings and a big sweater. This is much more comfortable than just James' t-shirt with nothing underneath, but I miss having his scent around me. I hope he comes home soon.

"Okay, so now that you have everything, you should be all set for another week or so. By then, your foot should be healed, and we can go shopping!" she says excitedly. I just nod my head, getting increasingly tired by the minute.

She talks for about another ten minutes while we sit on the bed. She talks about Dave and James, how they have been friends forever, and how much she is glad me and she can be friends.

"We were all a part of the pack growing up. Dave and I were friends, but most werewolf kids in our school don't to really mess around with each other because when we all got old enough, we didn't want to upset our mates. James has been waiting since he turned sixteen and didn't find you. He has spent the last six years waiting and looking for you." Hazel looks down, looking a bit sad. "It was a bit rough for him then. Most of us were mates and had a feeling but didn't quite know. Others found their mates within a couple of years. James just turned 22, and it was starting to show how upset he was when he still hadn't found his mate. He was convinced something had happened to you and you had died at a young age or were in a completely different country."

I am a little confused because I thought all mates would cross paths if they were still alive. She looks up and sees me confused before explaining more.

"If both mates are alive, then you will eventually cross paths. The only bad part is you don't really know when or how. James thought he would have to wait years, and that thought haunted him. He wanted to be with you; he was even planning to go over to Europe and Asia to travel and try to find you. It promised more hope than assuming you had died. That's usually the reason people don't find their soul mates. They have probably died from other causes before they got the chance to meet. The werewolf community is vast, but it's not that big. With all the things that help you recognize your mate, you really only have to be in the same building to smell them," she says while judging my reaction.

I nod and just look down at my hands. I feel bad for all the years James spent having to wonder where I was or if I was even out there. I am glad I am with him now, but after I was taken, I never thought about the werewolf community, or if I had a mate. My parents referred to each other as mates when I was younger, but I never got to the age where things like that were explained.

I'm glad I have Hazel here to explain things.

During the week I was spending time with James, I've realized they are similar to the pack I was taken from. They aren't like the other wolves who took me. When I think about my old pack, it saddens me to know they are out there, but I wouldn't want them seeing me... how I am now. I can't face them yet, and I can't face the people responsible who might still live under that roof. I think I would like it here in James' pack, so I have decided to give it a try for now and make a home here.

"James just mind-linked me. He will be back in about ten minutes. He has one more paper to fill out quickly, and he will be up."

I nod my head, getting a little more excited now.

"And just so you know, Grace, he told me about you not wanting to talk about what happened. I know it's scary and probably very hard to discuss, but if you ever want to talk, I'm here, okay? We are friends now, and I want you to know you can talk to me about anything at any time if you need to."

I nod, tears brimming in my eyes. She leans over and gives me a small hug before leaning back and stepping off the bed.

She walks over to a still sleeping Callie and picks her upright as James walks in the door. When he looks over at me and sees my hair, he stops in his tracks. I don't know if it's the hair or the clothes or even my new pink toenails, but for about another 30 seconds, he just stands in the doorway staring at me.

After a minute or so, I start fidgeting my hands, and my face starts to heat up. Why is he looking at me for that long?

"James?" Hazel says. "Are you going to stand there, or are you going to tell her how beautiful she looks?" She laughs a little.

He growls slightly at her mocking tone but walks over to sit next to me.

"Okay well, you two have fun. Remember what I said, Grace. Just have James call me anytime." She walks out the door, shutting it on her way out.

"She is right, you know. You are absolutely gorgeous," he says while looking into my eyes. I can feel my face heat up, and I look down at my hands in my lap, unsure of what to do. He puts his hand under my chin and tilts my head up, so I am looking at him.

When I look up, he is smiling at me, but doesn't say anything else which I am grateful for; I am already embarrassed enough.

"Want to go get some dinner? I can make pasta," he says. I nod my head but then look towards the door.

Downstairs? With the pack down there?

"If you want, you can go down and meet some of the pack. They won't all be down right now. Most of the teenagers are going out because it's

Friday, and the parents have their own pack house. The pack is too big to put all in one house."

I looked at him confused.

They can't be that big, can they? I haven't seen anyone other than Cassidy, Brittany, and Hazel.

"They aren't allowed to come up here. I told them not to. In total, we have a little over 2,000 members."

At this, my heart rate picked up considerably.

2,000! Where have they all been hiding? I start scooting back away on the bed until I felt myself close to the edge.

I can't meet the entire pack! That's so many people!

"Grace? Princess? Are you okay?" James worriedly scoots over and scoops me up in his arms. Once there, I can feel myself calm down, and I grab onto his shirt, burying my head in his chest.

After a minute or so of sitting like this, I look up at him and towards the door, debating if I want to go down or not.

"I just talked to Cole, and he says there are only around ten people in the kitchen right now. They are all mated besides Cole. Nobody will come near you besides the girls, you know. Hazel is down there, too."

I slowly nod, and we head out the door and down the stairs.

***

When we make it down, I switch around, so I am riding on his back. He doesn't seem to mind, and I feel better this way. When we walk into the kitchen, everybody turns to face me. I bury my head in James' back and silently hope none of them will come near me.

James moves over and sits on the countertop, putting me in his lap.

"Hey, Grace. Would you like some pasta for dinner? We were all just about to eat." I hear Hazel and look over to see her in the kitchen with Brittany and another girl. They are cooking a lot of pasta. I nod my head and give her a small smile which she returns. She then turns around to stir the sauce.

When I turn around, a couple of people are looking over at me curiously. Sitting on the opposite of the two couples that I don't recognize are Dave and Cole from the woods, and sitting next to them are two other men.

"Well, Grace. You remember Dave and Cole, right?"

I nod my head, and they give me a small smile.

James introduces me to the others. The bigger of the two boys is Caiden. He is Brittany's mate. He appears to be an inch or so shorter than James and has blonde hair that contrasts Brittany's small frame and black hair.

The other man is Mac. He is the shortest of the guys but is still around 6 feet, and his mate is the other girl in the kitchen, Emma, who is about the same height as me. They both have blonde hair.

The couples sitting off to the side are Rose, Jackson, Cassidy, and Ethan. Cassidy is the girl who cut my hair. She is slightly taller than me and has brown hair. Her mate is Ethan who is the same height and body build as Caiden, but Ethan has a dirty blond hair leaning more towards light brown.

Rose and Jackson are the last couple. Rose is the tallest of the girls and has blonde hair, while Jackson, who told me to call him Jack, has jet black hair and is also very tall and built like Caiden and Ethan.

Once introductions are over, the food is ready, and we go and sit at the table with everybody else. James sits at the end of the table, I sit to his right, and Cole sits to his left. Hazel sits on my right with Dave next to her, and the rest fill in down the table, sitting next to their respective mates.

"So, Grace, I was thinking the girls could come with us shopping next week. They can help us pick out so many outfits: summer outfits and winter outfits…"

I just nod at Hazel as she talks and the girls pipe into the conversation.

I am grateful that nobody brings up how I got here or why James carries me everywhere. I am also happy nobody asks why, after only a couple bites, I feel like I am stuffed. But above all, I am really grateful that nobody asks why I don't talk.

Chapter 13

After dinner, everybody helps clean up while James pulls me into his lap whispering in my ear about how happy he is that I met his friends. He thinks me going out with the girls next week will be fun. I just sit there and nod my head, listening to his voice while my hands play with his hands in front of me and my head lie back on his shoulder.

After a few minutes, everybody goes into the living room to watch a movie, while Hazel and Dave say they are going to check on Callie, who is still asleep from this afternoon.

All the girls say how excited they are to go shopping and say goodbye before they all head off to the living room, leaving James and me sitting at the table.

James turns me around to face him, and I blush at how close our faces are. Maybe he will kiss me again. But do I want him to kiss me again?

Yes.

"Do you want to go watch the movie or head back up?" he asks, staring into my eyes.

I just shrug my shoulder.

"Well, you have had a very eventful day with Hazel and dinner, so why don't we go back up and we can hang out for a little before bed?" I nod my head, and he stands up with me in his arms. My arms are around his neck and my legs wrapped around his waist.

***

Once we make it upstairs, he puts me on the bed and starts a movie called *Finding Nemo*. I am pretty sure I remember seeing this before.

When James comes back to the bed, he sits against the headboard. He reaches over, and before I can think about it, I flinch back. He gets this hurt look and pulls his arms back, facing towards the movie. I feel guilty. I actually do want to sit with him. It was just a reflex, and I didn't mean to hurt his feelings. I crawl over, sit in between his legs, and lean back against his chest. When he doesn't move, I grab his arms and place them around my waist.

Once I settle in, I feel him relax against me. I can't concentrate on the movie, and I become very aware of how close he is to me.

Does he like sitting like this? Would he want to kiss me?

I turn around in his lap and face him, straddling his waist. When I look into his eyes, he is staring at me, slightly confused.

"You okay, princess?" he asks.

I lift my hand up and place it against the side of his face. I can feel his slight stubble starting to grow in along his face, and I suddenly wonder how it would feel against my face if we kissed. I feel my cheeks heat up as I realize what I was just thinking. Why would he want to kiss me? I am damaged. He just stays with me because the mate bond makes him want to.

At this thought, my eyes water; this whole week we have become close, and I trust him now. I didn't think I would ever want to be involved with another man. I think I like him, but I don't even know what that is like. I didn't get the teenage experience of having my first crush or talking to boys. The men I was around with were dirty and did what they wanted without any care that I was a person. They didn't care if they were hurting and using me.

When he sees my eyes water, he grabs my face with his hands and wipes the tears away before they can escape.

"You have to tell me what's wrong, baby. Let me fix it. What's going through your mind?" He waits for my response though knowing I probably won't talk.

I slowly lean in to kiss him but stop a couple of inches away from his face.

When he doesn't move away, I lean in further, and then our lips connect. I feel those same sparks I feel every time we touch, but they suddenly become stronger. We start kissing, our lips moving in sync, when he licks my bottom lip. I don't know how to do any of this, but I open my mouth, and the kiss gets deeper. Our tongues go back and forth in a sort of dance.

When the kiss starts to get heated, he pulls away and looks at me

"Princess, don't get me wrong. I love kissing you, but I don't know how much I can hold myself or my wolf back and I don't know how much you are ready for." He tucks a strand of hair behind my ear while looking into my eyes.

I run my finger over his lips and kiss him one more time before turning back around. He lays us back down, and we watch the movie before going to bed.

***

The weekend passes uneventfully. James and I now both sleep in the bed every night, with me tucked under his arm, feeling safe and secure. I saw Hazel and Callie a couple more times, but it wasn't until Monday that we spent the day together again. Some of the other girls also show up for a bit to bring food and stuff, and we went to a living room somewhere on James' floor to watch movies. We made a plan to go shopping on Wednesday since I have to go and see Doctor Richards again about my leg and foot today.

The stitches should be falling out soon, but my foot is still sore to bear any weight. I can sort of hop around, and if I walk on my toes, it isn't too bad. James still gets upset when he sees me trying to walk, though. He says I should be resting and not hurting myself more.

"Okay, angel, I just need to grab you a coat and then we can go." James has been hovering over every little thing. It's nice that he cares, but it's a bit ridiculous. I learned it is already October from Hazel, which means it's only fall and it shouldn't even be getting really cold until the end of November. I would like to see someone convince James of that. He is convinced that I need layers before I can go out.

James walks over to his closet and grabs one of his massive sweatshirts, puts it on me, and we are out the door minutes later. The walk is peaceful. I look around and notice all of the younger children playing outside. It's easy to spot the mothers because they are all in a group hovering nearby, watching the little kids carefully. I smile as I watch them all from a distance.

When I look back up, I see James looking down at me smiling.

"Maybe you can meet some more of the pack next week," he says. "If you want to, that is," he adds when he sees my face.

I shrug my shoulders, still slightly scared of meeting his pack. There are so many people in it, I don't think I can handle that. Not to mention James said he had to mark me before I meet the rest of them and I am definitely not ready for that.

Minutes later, we are walking into the doctor's office, and he is leading us to a room.

After looking at my foot and thigh, the doctor says the cut on my foot and the gash on my thigh are almost completely healed. The cut is closed, and the stitches are almost all out, but it will be sore to walk on. He asks me to walk around a bit to see how much it hurts.

"How does that feel?"

I just put a thumb up. My foot hurts a little but not nearly as much as before.

"Okay, good. I want to see you about every couple of weeks for normal checkups. I don't know how much you and Alpha James have talked about this, but you need to be gaining weight. You have gained about 3 pounds in the week or so that you have been here, which is good. I know it's hard to eat a lot because your body still needs to adjust. I need you to be eating all three meals a day. Can you do that for me?"

I nod, and he smiles.

"Thank you, Richard. We will see you in a couple weeks," James says. He leads me outside, and we slowly make our way back to the house. I don't let James carry me. I want to walk; I haven't been able to walk for the past week.

***

Once we get to the house, we walk to the kitchen to get some lunch. I notice not a lot of people are in the house. It's too quiet for a bunch of teenagers to be living here.

When James looks over and sees me confused, he starts to speak, "I told everyone to stay in the lounges and games rooms upstairs and to stay clear of the hallways unless they need something. I didn't want any of them scaring you now that you are more comfortable around us." He admits, looking down.

We stop right before the doorway to the kitchen, and I turn to face him. I nod my head and interlace my fingers with his, grabbing his hand. Sometimes, I forget how big he is until I stand next to him. I look down, and you can barely even see my hand when it is surrounded by his hand. I look up at his face, and I really have to tilt my head back to look up at him. Then I realize I don't even make it to his shoulder. I look up at his face again and pout.

I don't like being so small.

"What's wrong, angel?" He calls me so many nicknames and pet names. I just shake my head in response.

"What is it?" He is looking down at me, and my head is just about to make it to his chest. I lift my hand up and place it at my height. I then reach up my other hand to his height although I can barely reach his forehead. I hold them both out, so I am comparing our heights. Once he understands, it's like a light bulb went off behind his eyes.

"Angel, I love your height. You are small, and it makes me feel like I can protect you. I like it, and it's not a big deal to me anyways. You could be taller than me for all I care as long as I have you."

I look down at all of my now fading bruises and cuts and frown again. How can he like me? I'm so ugly.

"Grace..." He lifts my chin, so my eyes meet his. "They don't matter. That's a part of your past. It shows me how strong you are to have endured what you did. Don't worry about it, and if anybody has a problem with it, they can talk to me, and I'll be sure to straighten them out."

I hear a noise that has me gripping onto James' shirt and hiding behind him.

"Aww!"

I turn around at the sudden high pitched squeals. I see Rose, Emma, Cassidy, and Brittany sitting at the table with Hazel in the kitchen making Callie's lunch. My heart beat is going a mile a minute. I didn't even see them in here!

"Princess, it's alright. It's just the girls." He pulls me out from behind him and continues talking. "It's actually a good thing you girls are here." He looks back down at me. "Would you mind hanging out with them for the afternoon? I have some more work that I have to catch up on. I'll come back around dinner time, okay?"

I nod my head, and he kisses my forehead before walking off to his office.

I turn around, and I see six pairs of eyes looking at me, smiling.

Chapter 14

The girls and I all sit down and eat lunch together. They made a bunch of mac and cheese, and afterward, we clean up and decide to watch a movie in the living room. Hazel goes to put Callie for her afternoon nap and then joins us in the living room.

After the first movie, the girls put in another movie. I think this is a scary movie because it is called *Paranormal Activity*. The beginning starts out kind of slow, so after about ten minutes, the girls turn to me and smile. I look back confused. Hazel is the first to speak.

"So you seem a lot more comfortable around James now," she says, smiling at me. I nod my head, still wondering where this is going.

"So have you guys kissed?" Brittany throws in. I blush when I think of the nights right before bed where we usually kiss for a couple of minutes.

"Ohhh, my gosh!" They all squeal.

I just start laughing, covering my flaming face with my hands.

"So, you kind of like him now, huh?" Rose asks.

My face gets even more red if that's even possible. I shrug.

We are soul mates for a reason. James said if we got to know each other, there would be no one else in the world who could understand me better than he will. I have to give him a chance. Otherwise, I could be missing out on the one person who could be my perfect match. He has been really nice to me and has helped me the second I need something. He is one of the very few people I have trusted in a long time, and I hope it continues this way.

But then again, he could turn at any moment. I just don't know what to expect. A small part of me is telling me that he would never hurt me, and another part of me is reminding me of my past.

They notice my distant look and start talking about what store they plan on going to tomorrow. I have never heard of any of them before now, but that's not a surprise. After about twenty minutes, it falls silent again, and we watch the movie.

An hour later into the movie, things get a little too scary for me that I hide behind a blanket with Hazel on one side of me and Emma on the other. The rest of the girls are on the other couch under their blankets. Something is about to pop out, I can tell, so I cover half of my face behind my hands, peeking my eyes out just enough to see.

"Hey, girls!" The second we hear that, we all scream and jump up before hiding under our blankets.

I can feel myself shaking along with Hazel and Emma. We all have a death grip on each other, still freaking out.

"Girls, girls, it's okay. It's just us!" Someone pulls back the blanket, and we scream again.

I look up and see Dave and Mac standing over us while Caiden, Jackson, and Ethan are in front of the other couch, pulling the girls from their blanket. Once I see it's them, I try to calm down, but my heart is going so fast.

The girls jump into their mate's arms, and I stay on the couch, trying to breathe.

"Grace, are you okay?" I look over, and Cole is in the doorway, staring at me. I just nod my head and look down while trying to breathe. "Do you need me to get James? He is right upstairs."

I just shake my head. I can't lose it because of a scary movie. It was just a movie. The guys weren't even trying to scare us.

Breathe. Grace just breathe. Just a movie. Just the guys. You are okay.

Hazel sits back down next to me and rubs my back gently.

A couple of minutes later, my breathing is back to normal, and my heart rate has slowed down. I look up at everybody and smile while they are still looking at me concerned.

"So how about no scary movies for a while?" Hazel suggests, and I laugh a little. The tension in the room is broken as everyone else laughs too.

A couple of minutes later, everyone is sitting down on the couches and talking while I sit and listen. Shortly afterwards, James comes through the doorway, and I jump up and hug him really tightly.

"You alright, angel?" I just nod at him, and bury my face in his chest. "Hazel?" He turns to Hazel in concern.

"Nothing. We just watched a scary movie and the guys walked in and scared us on accident," Hazel says.

He looks back down at me. "You okay, angel?" I nod again, and he hugs me. He picks me up and brings me to the kitchen. "You hungry?" he asks.

I just shrug my shoulders. The girls and I ate about 4 or 5 hours ago, so I'm not really hungry.

"Grace, you heard Doctor Richard. You have to eat three meals a day at least. Come on, I'll make you a sandwich." He sets me on one of the stools and starts getting stuff to make my sandwich.

I just watch his body as he walks around the kitchen with a face pinched in concentration while making the sandwich. I watch his muscles flex as he moves. I am still looking at James when I hear him start to chuckle.

"See something you like, princess?" He doesn't even look up at me, but I can hear the smirk in his voice. Realizing I was being creepy, my face gets beet red, and I look down and fiddle with my hands in my lap.

"It's okay, sweetheart. You can look all you want. This is all yours." Smirking now, he comes over and puts a plate in front of me while taking his plate and sitting down. My face gets even hotter and is probably about the color of a tomato right now.

Great.

Just great.

Chapter 15

The next day, the girls and I head out right after breakfast to start our shopping. James gives me his credit card and tells me to buy whatever I need and not to worry about the cost. But there is no way I am spending all of his money.

I'll buy an outfit or two.

With that, we head off to the local mall.

***

Three hours and many bags later, we are all exhausted. Thank god we have guards with us carrying the bags.

James and Dave insisted we take at least one guard for each of us and then they added two extra. I was introduced to them this morning at breakfast, and James made it clear to each of them not to come close to me or touch me unless I am in danger. I looked at him gratefully because there were a lot of guys with us and I couldn't handle it if they come near me. I am sure they are all perfectly nice, but there are just so many of them.

Cole came with us, which makes me feel a little better. He has been going in all of the stores with us and talking to us. The rest of them split up. Some comes inside the store while the others wait outside. They keep to themselves and only helps when we ask, so they aren't too scary.

"Rose, we need to stop and eat lunch, or I'm going to fall over!" Hazel exclaims. Rose is the shopaholic, I have learned, and wants to keep going, but the rest of us are exhausted.

"One last store and then we can go get food."

I look up and see we are in front of a store that says Victoria's Secret. Exactly like all of the other stores, I have never heard of this one before, and I wonder what's here that we couldn't have found anywhere else.

I look into the store we are walking into and realize that underwear and bras are everywhere!

Oh no!

I make a move to turn around and walk out when Brittany grabs my arm.

"No way, Grace. You need some of this stuff. And don't you want to get a couple of cute things for James?" she says with a wink.

I blush at that. Would James even want to see me in this?

We shop around, and the girls make me buy a couple of thongs even though I have never worn one. Personally, I think they look completely uncomfortable. They also have me fitted for bras, and we grab some of those as well.

Afterward, we head to a different section that looks more scandalous.

"Grace, you need at least two matching sets of these, and then we can leave," says Hazel. I nod my head and look over some racks as the girls help me look.

"Oh, Grace, what about this one?" Cassidy comes over, holding up a bra that has some shear material down the front that makes it look like a tank top. I gasp as I can see right through it. Along with it is a matching thong.

I just nod my head knowing the faster I get them, the faster we can get out of this store. Emma comes over holding one similar item. The only difference is the color; it's black and pink and it looks like it has straps attached to... socks? That can't be right. Who would wear this under clothes?

Hazel looks at me and explains that these are outfits for our more intimate times and they aren't really things you wear on a daily basis. I blush beet red and shake my head no, but the girls insist I get these, and I give in, knowing I am going to lose this argument. I just want to get out of this section as soon as possible. Hazel explains the straps everywhere, and I nod my head and take the sets they have picked out. After paying, we walk out of the store and see all the guys sitting around looking uncomfortable. One steps forward to grab my bag and then we all turn to head to the food court.

After eating, we shop for accessories and shoes. The shoes take a long time because I have to try every pair and a lot of the time, we have to find the smallest size in the women's section. The girls convince me to get some jewelry and necklaces, and I agree to save time.

I am really grateful that they are here to help me pick my clothes. I haven't had a chance in a really long time to make decisions for myself about what I can wear and what I can get.

Being able to buy things and choose my outfits and styles is very liberating. I get to choose who I want to be and how I want to look for a change. The girls suggested many different styles and helped me find the type of clothes that I like. Overall, it was a fun day, and it was nice to be around the girls and to feel accepted by them. I think all of us are going to be very close. During the car ride home, the girls sing along to a bunch of songs, and soon, we are pulling up to the house.

Once we all get out of the cars, the boys take all my bags and bring them in the house. I try to grab a couple, but they refuse, so I grab the Victoria's Secret bag quickly while another guard shuts the trunk. I don't need them seeing what I bought.

When I get to James' room, I see all of the bags next to the walk-in closet. I wonder where he wants me to put all those items I have bought.

"Hey, angel, how did your shopping go?"

I jump at the sound of his voice. I turn to face him, putting a hand over my heart.

"Oh, sorry, sweetheart. I didn't mean to scare you." He comes over to me slowly and wraps his arms around me, kissing the top of my head.

I hug him back tight and then let go before walking over to put the Victoria's Secret bag behind the rest of the bags.

"Do you want help putting your stuff away?" he asks. I shrug my shoulders, and when he leads me into the closet carrying the bags, I look and see that half the closet is empty.

"I always kept one side empty for whenever I found my mate," he says quietly.

I look over at him; he was really waiting for me to come around? Now I feel bad he got stuck with someone like me. I don't deserve someone as great as him.

Looking down, I avoid eye contact and start pulling things out of the bags. I mainly got dresses and leggings along with big sweaters; since winter is coming up, we didn't shop for summer clothes. The girls said we could do that in the spring. A lot of the sweaters and shirts were big even if they weren't supposed to be because of how small I am. The girls offered to go to the girl's section to look for t-shirts and long sleeve shirts that might fit me, but I didn't want to do that. I like the bigger clothes anyways, and they are warmer.

The girls made me buy a lot of things. It feels like a lot, and I am folding so many pairs of pants, it's ridiculous. I bought one pair of jeans that fit the best, but they were still loose and didn't fit right. After folding, I look and see James has hung up a lot of shirts. I start pulling the shoes out of the bags, and I put them on the floor under the racks of clothes. When I got to the jewelry, I didn't know where to put it, so I kept it all in one bag and put it on the shelf.

I do feel bad about buying a lot of stuff, but this the bare minimum of what they would let me buy. I definitely spent a lot on all of this, but they wouldn't take no for an answer!

James is helping me unpack and hang everything up. He looks over at me and smiles. I look at him sheepishly and look back at the bags. I shouldn't have bought so much.

"So this is a good start of clothing. I'm sure the girls will want to go again in the next couple weeks. Those girls always need something new." He chuckles.

A good start? I don't know how much more I can buy without spending all of his money.

I reach into my, well his, sweatshirt pocket and pull out the credit card and hand it back to him. I cannot spend any more of his money.

"Just keep that one. You will need it next time and if you do other things with the girls and I'm not there. I have a few more I can use. It's okay, sweetheart."

I look at him, bewildered. I hold the credit card to him again. There is no way I am keeping this.

"Grace, look at me." I look up into his chocolate eyes. "That's yours now, okay? Money is not an issue. You can buy whatever you need with that card. Don't be scared of buying too much because I have plenty of money. The pack owns several companies and things that are in this town. My family runs its own accounting firm to help people in the pack, and we occasionally help humans too. The alphas also get paid for running the pack. We are more than comfortable financially, and I don't want you to worry about anything. The girls told me how you didn't want to buy more than one shirt, but I'm telling you I'm surprised they only let you buy this little." He laughs at that part but then sobers up quickly. "Grace, I'm serious. Don't ever let money be an issue between us. It's my job to provide for you, and I always will."

I nod and look up at him. I can feel my eyes start to water.

Nobody has cared about me since I was taken from my family. Those men didn't care about what I needed at all. They never bought me a single thing the entire time I was there. I was only allowed a couple of meals a week.

He pulls me in for a hug and kisses the top of my head.

"What's wrong, princess?" he asks.

I just shake my head and look up at him, staring at his lips. I stand on my toes and even with that, I have to wait until he leans down and gently presses his lips to mine. We pull away, and he wipes the tears that started to fall down my face.

We finish up hanging shirts, and when I look over at him, he is holding the Victoria's Secret bag.

"Grace?" he says, holding it up.

I run over and quickly snatch it away before putting it on a low shelf behind some folded leggings. He does not need to see that right now.

He chuckles a little. I turn around. My face is once again red.

"Will I get to see those soon?" he asks.

At this, I freeze. Does he expect that soon? Is that why the girls wanted me to get those things? I don't know how long until I can even consider being that intimate with James. The only experience I have of sex or being close to another person, if you can even call it that, was with those men who took me from my family.

Before I know it, tears have formed in my eyes again. I'm terrified of what's going to happen.

"Grace? Ah, shit." James starts coming over to me. He pulls me into a hug. "I didn't mean we have to anytime soon.. or ever if you don't really want to. That will be difficult, but if that's what you want. Having you in my life is more important than anything else. Even if it takes years of just being friends or if you don't want to change the way we are now, I can do that. I will wait however long you think you need. I don't want to pressure you into anything you don't want and please, don't feel like you have to, okay? I have never done that with a girl anyways, so it's not like I'm missing out, right?" He jokes at the end. I just stare at him confused.

Has he never been with a girl? I look back at him, and he looks embarrassed, and I see a slight tint of pink to his cheeks.

"I wanted to wait for my mate. I wanted it to be special and for her to know she is the only one I care enough to... be intimate with. I imagine if humans knew they had soul mates, they would wait, too. There is something about knowing there is someone out there for me. I didn't want to ruin it by sleeping with some random person when I knew I would find you one day. I wanted it to be our moment that nobody else got to share. I mean, the guys all assume I have been with one of the girls we used to hang around in high school, but I never did. I knew no one would compare to my mate."

He is way too good for me. I don't deserve him. He deserves so much better. I'm used. I'm dirty, and he doesn't even know it, and when he does, he will be crushed. He will want me to leave; I wouldn't blame him if he did. I don't deserve the good life he could give me.

I start shaking my head back and forth and sit on the ground crying.

Why did this happen to me? I can't even give my mate the very thing he wanted. It was already taken from me.

What is wrong with me?

"Hey, hey, shhh… It's okay, Grace. What's wrong? Tell me, and I'll fix it." He thinks he can fix things and fix me. He thinks we will have this perfect life now that he has found his soul mate. But he can't because it's me. I'm the damaged one, and there is nothing he can do to give me back what they stole. That will forever be ingrained in my mind, and once he knows, he won't be okay with that, after everything he has done for me.

I start shaking my head back and forth, and he tries to calm me down again. "What's wrong? Tell me, and I'll fix it," he says again.

I shake my head, and after almost a decade, I utter two words.

"I'm broken."

Chapter 16

He gasps as he hears me speak, and it goes dead silent for about two seconds. I wait for the backlash; for the hit or slap, but it never comes.

"Grace?" he says softly. I look back up at his face to see tears in his eyes. "Did you just speak? Was that you?" he asks as if he doesn't believe me, as if there is a ghost in the room.

I just nod my head and put my head back on my knees, curling up into a ball. I should just spare him the trouble of having to kick me out. I should leave and make it easier for him. He deserves better. If I can get out of here quick enough or within a couple of hours, I can make some decent ground before anyone can try and stop me or ask why I'm leaving.

That's even if I make it more than a couple of hours without running into other wolves, and who knows what will happen if I run into others. No pack is going to want me after hearing about me. I'm a burden to anyone who would to take me in.

"Princess, what do you mean broken? Tell me what's wrong. I want to fix it," he says. He even sounds convincing; like he will actually want me to stay around after he hears about this.

"Grace, I think now is a good time to talk about what happened to you, don't you think? It sounds like a lot to hold in and deal with on your own, and I want you to be able to confide in me. I think it's important for me to know where you came from or why you have bruises and scars from so long ago." I just stay silent. "Please, princess, I need to know," he begs while leaning his head on my shoulder. We are now sitting on the ground, me curled up in a ball and him wrapping himself around me. Why he even wants to be near me or wants to be touching me, is a mystery to me.

"They took me," I whisper. I lift my head up and see him looking at me, completely concentrated on what I'm saying.

"Who took you?"

I don't answer. Talking feels so weird, and my voice is very hoarse.

"Did they take you from your house?"

I nod.

"Did they take you from your pack?"

I nod again.

"Well, maybe we can find your pack and tell them you are okay. I'm sure they are wondering where you are by now."

I start crying again. I doubt they are looking for me. It's been about ten years, they probably gave up and moved on.

"How long did they have you?" he asks quietly.

"Ten years I think, maybe a little less than that." I shrug.

"How did you get away?" he asks.

"I don't know really. It was all so fast. I was doing my chores, making them food, and they started arguing, then fighting, and then the leader killed one of the guys. The rest started to fight, and I went to try and get out. Nobody was watching me. The leader either killed the others or saw me leave and stopped fighting with them to come after me. He was yelling taunts in the woods, and when he caught up to me, he dragged me back to the house and told me everything he planned on doing. I was so frustrated and sad that I almost got away again and failed at it, and before I knew it, I was shifting. He came after me and got my leg with his claw. He was injured from fighting the others. I could tell because he was limping, so I took advantage and started fighting back. I eventually cut him across his neck. He fell as he struggled to breathe. I took off and didn't look back." I finish the story and look down.

"What were the things he was saying to you?" he asks.

I just keep my head down and shake my head. When he doesn't do anything, I look up and see his pitch-black eyes staring right at me.

Furious, he picks me up, walks out of the walk-in closet, and sits me on the edge of the bed. What surprises me is instead of lashing out, he sits me on the edge of the bed and starts pacing the room, running his hands through his hair roughly.

"What did they do to you, Grace?" I just look down. "Grace, tell me what they did! I am going to kill them. I am going to kill them all. I swear, I'm going to kill them." He keeps mumbling about death while I watch him get increasingly worked up.

"Did they hurt you, Grace?" I just nod, looking down. He punches the wall next to the closet.

"They kept you chained like some animal, didn't they?" I nod again, and a lamp goes flying off his desk in the corner.

I start to weep heavily, wondering if he is going to come for me next.

"Grace, did they… did they rape you?"

I keep my head down and slowly nod my head. I start crying louder and curl myself into a ball. I can feel my heartbeat going too fast, and I am starting to have a hard time breathing.

Next thing I hear is the desk flying across the room

Please stop. Please…

I say this over and over in my head. Suddenly, the door opens, Hazel and Dave stand in the doorway with Brittany and Caiden, and a confused Cole follows behind them. I am sobbing uncontrollably, finding every second even more difficult to breathe.

Hazel looks around the room and sees that almost everything is broken. She looks at me crying and then at James who is still punching and destroying things.

"James!" Dave yells.

James looks over to see the group of people standing in the doorway. They slowly move into the room. I look over and see James' eyes are obsidian, completely black with no hint of their warm chocolate color to them.

"James, please calm down. You need to calm down," Hazel slowly says. She makes a move to come to me, and he growls and steps towards her in front of me. I can barely breathe, and I'm making a wheezing sound now.

"James, look at what you are doing. You are scaring Grace. Whatever it is, we can talk about it! We can fix it, but you need to calm down and let me see her."

He growls and makes a step towards her. Dave quickly steps in front of Hazel, protecting her from him. My vision is starting to have black dots everywhere, and I realize that I am going to pass out in a couple of minutes.

"James, calm down. Hey, James, look at Grace. Lok at your mate! She can't breathe. You are scaring her too much. You need to let us help. You need to let us see her before she passes out or worse... Just look at her, James..."

After that, I think I see James turning around, but I can't be sure because a second later, everything goes black.

Chapter 17

Beep. Beep. Beep.

I wake up to hear a weird beeping noise and to my head feeling heavy like a rock. Trying to pry my eyes open, I feel someone holding my hand. I try and squeeze it, but my whole body feels weak.

I hear someone's footsteps approaching, and I still haven't opened my eyes.

"Alpha James, you really should get some rest. She will wake up soon..." I hear Dr. Richards say.

"It's been a whole day. Why hasn't she woken up yet, Richard? I have to be here when she wakes up," he says angrily.

I hear the Doctor mumble a response and then his retreating footsteps. I need to get up. James doesn't want me here. I am just another problem. I try to open my eyes, and I feel them flutter open before light blinds me. I close them again, groaning.

"Princess? Are you awake?" He sounds almost hopeful. "Doctor, Richard! Get back in here. She is waking up!" James suddenly yells.

I hear a couple pairs of footsteps run into my room and feel someone poking and prodding at me. Someone grabs my other hand.

"Grace, are you there? Try to open your eyes, squeeze my hand if you want, but do something."

My head feels fuzzy, and I feel disoriented, but I manage to open my eyes.

I get blinded by the light above me. Where the hell am I?

I open my eyes more and see that James is sitting next to me in a chair, with bags under his eyes and Dr. Richards next to him, staring at me intently.

"Take it easy. What do you remember, Grace?" he asks.

I think about it for a minute, and I remember shopping with the girls, all of those embarrassing lingerie from Victoria's Secret, and James flipping things over. I look over at James, and my heart rate picks up. I can hear the beeping going faster as I realize why I passed out.

"Grace, it's okay. I'm sorry. I shouldn't have scared you like that. I promise I will never hurt you. I swear," he says with a sad look on his face. I take my hand out of his, and his frown deepens. Sadness is etched all over his face.

Why am I still here? He could have just kicked me out while I was sleeping.

"Grace." I look over and see Dr. Richards staring at me. "You had a panic attack, and you have been asleep for 24 hours. Otherwise, you are fine. Your body just went into shock for a bit. Your mind was reminded of the violence you have faced and kept you asleep while you recovered," he says calmly. He hesitates before starting again. "Grace, you have been doing well and have been eating, but your body still isn't getting much stronger. You need to be on a strict diet of foods that are good for you and will give you the nutrients you need."

I nod my head as I listen and wait for them to tell me I need to leave, that they don't want me.

"Okay. Well, you should get some rest, and I can probably let you go tonight or early tomorrow morning."

I nod my head again.

"Thank you, Richard." I hear James say.

I just stare straight forward, preparing myself. This would have been so much easier if he just let me go while I was out. I don't think I can handle him rejecting me.

"Babe, you had me so worried about you." He confesses and buries his head in my lap.

Stunned, I just stare at him. I pat his head awkwardly, not knowing what to do. I was not expecting this. I was expecting disgust, or anger or violence, but never for him to be this worried about me.

"Grace, please just talk to me. I know you can." I shake my head back and forth. I did, and he started throwing things. He doesn't want to hear what I have to say. He sits up and grabs my hands in his before I can pull away.

What on Earth is he doing?

"Grace, if you think that in any way I am mad at you, I'm not. This wasn't your fault. None of it was."

I just look away from him with tears in my eyes. I can't take this anymore. I don't want to talk about it. The memories themselves are enough without reminders.

"Grace, listen to me." He pulls my chin to look up at him. "I will protect you. I meant it when I said that. Nobody will ever force you into anything again. Nobody will be taking you away again, and I will personally make sure of that," he says. He sounds convincing.

"Listen to what I have to say next. You are not broken. You are perfect, you are beautiful, and you are strong, and I will take however long it takes to prove that to you." He leans over and kisses my forehead.

Isn't he going to make me leave?

I look up at him with tears freely going down my face now. "Why?" I mumble quietly.

"Because, Grace, I am your mate. I will always want to protect you. I will always take care of you. I meant everything I said before. You are my life now, and I will take care of everything and anything you need. You are mine. I am yours. And it's going to be like that for the rest of our lives." He says the last part while tucking a strand of hair behind my ear.

I grab onto him as he leans over the bed and hugs me gently while I cry into his shoulder.

Why am I so lucky to get someone like him?

***

The doctor lets me go back to James' house with him but says I still need to rest and eat a lot of food.

Our walk back to the house is silent, and when we get there, we head up to the room for bed. Once I have showered, I grab some PJ's and get into bed. James comes out ten minutes later wearing some basketball shorts.

When I look at his face, he is already looking at me, smiling. I quickly look away and turn around to my other side, wishing the ground would just swallow me up whole before I die of embarrassment. I am always getting flustered around him.

The lights shut off, and seconds later, I feel the covers being pulled up and an arm wrapping around my waist. James pulls me back, my back makes contact with his chest. I feel his breath at the back of my neck, and he trails his nose along my neck before placing a small kiss right behind my ear.

"Goodnight, princess," he murmurs.

I just hum back and smile to myself.

***

The next week passes relatively smoothly, unless you count James' freak out the next morning because I didn't want to talk. Since then, he hasn't pressured me to talk. Normally during the day, I hang out with Hazel or the girls, and around dinner time, James will finish his work for the day, and we will hang out in his room and watch movies.

The past week, I have been trying to avoid kissing him and being too touchy with him. I don't want to get too close to him because now, he knows I'm not the perfect mate he was hoping for. I want him to be happy, and it makes me feel guilty knowing he waited his entire life for me and I can't live up to his expectations. Not like it was my choice, but what can I do about it? Nothing.

I can see he gets frustrated when I pull away and don't answer his questions, but no matter what, he still tries to talk to me. He doesn't say anything about it, but every morning, I wake up in his arms no matter how many blankets and pillows I have put between us the night before.

It is now Sunday afternoon, and the girls and I are in the living room on James' floor, playing Candy Land with Callie. The boys are all out doing runs, and I am quickly getting bored of this game. Callie should be asleep by now, but she has boundless energy today. I look up and see the guys walking in early.

"Hey, girls. How's everything going?" James asks, and before I even realize it, he picks me up and sets me on his lap. I try and squirm around, trying to get off, when I realize I am rubbing myself all over him.

"Angel, I wouldn't squirm so much if I were you," he whispers in my ear. My face gets red while he chuckles in my ear. He kisses my neck and turns his attention to everybody as they listen to Callie talk about our day.

"…and we all made ice cream sundaes after lunch! Mommy let me put extra M&M's on mine, Daddy!" She runs and jumps on Dave.

"I can see that, sweetie," Dave says as he sits next to Hazel. "Well, how about you, Mommy, and I spend the rest of the day together?" he asks while looking down.

She cheers and jumps up while grabbing both of their hands, towing them out of the room. They turn and wave to the rest of us while walking out.

One by one, the couples slowly leave the room until it's just James and me.

"What about you, angel? Want to spend the rest of the day with me?" I just shrug my shoulders, and he gets up with me still in his arms. He walks towards the bedroom and sits us down on the bed with me still on his lap.

"I want to talk to you about something." I nod my head. "So, my parents and my sister have wanted to meet you for some time now, but I kept telling them no. I didn't want you to feel pressured, and I wanted us to be closer and know each other a little more than we do right now. I was wondering if you would want to meet them this week. And then this weekend, I can introduce you as my mate to the pack..." He trails off.

I just stare at him dumbfounded. All of them want to meet me? Why?

"If you aren't ready, that's fine. I can push it back to another couple of weeks, but they are growing impatient to meet their new luna." He pauses for a second. "But there is one condition."

I look at him curiously. What is he talking about?

"I need to mark you before you can meet the pack."

Chapter 18

"Would that be okay? We don't have to do anything else, but I need the pack to know you are mine and that you're off limits. This will keep you safe from them. They wouldn't dare hurt you once you're marked. I mean… not that they would anyway. My pack is very respectful, but just to be safe. It is more about so they will know your rank and that I'm your mate and show you respect. They are all very nice and are looking forward to finally meeting you. Once they meet you and you become luna, they will always respect you and protect you no matter what." He stares at me while I take this in.

I was told that when he marks me, we would both feel the need to finish the mating process. Our hormones will be going crazy, and both the mating and the marking usually happen simultaneously. As soon as he marks me, I will officially be a part of this pack and the luna, or female leader of the pack.

Do I want him to mark me? That's permanent. I would love to spend the rest of my life with James; he is the perfect man, but does he really want to spend his life stuck with me? Is he only doing this for my protection?

"Grace, what's going on? What are you thinking?" I shrug my shoulders and just stare at him.

"Don't do this because of my safety," I whisper, but I know he heard me.

"Baby, no! That's not what I meant. I really want to do it. I have wanted to do it since I met you, but I didn't want to upset you or try anything until you were ready. Since the pack is very big, I just thought it would make you feel better. I'm sorry, I didn't mean it like that. I would love to mark you, show the world that you are my mate and my girlfriend, but I didn't know how you felt about it and that's why I'm asking now."

I just stare at him.

Did he just call me his girlfriend? He wants me to be his girlfriend?

"I-I m-mean, I-I didn't mean girlfriend... u-unless that's what you want. It's totally up to you!" He rushes the end of the sentence out. After everything he discovered about me, he still wants to be with me?

I'm so happy, I want to cry, but I have cried so much already, so instead of answering him, I just push my hair behind my shoulders and stare at him until he realizes. I know I am falling for James, and we have really gotten close these past couple of weeks. I trust him, and if he still wants to be with me, I would be a fool to turn that down.

"R-Really? Grace, are you sure this is what you want? I don't want you to feel like you have to."

I nod my head and lean in until I am a couple of inches away. I can feel his breath on my lips, and I wait to see if he will kiss me.

A second later, I feel his lips on mine, and they start moving at a slow pace together. He licks my bottom lip, and the kiss deepens until we are both breathing heavy and our hands are all over each other. I move my hands to wrap them around his neck and tangle my hands in his hair. I feel his arms tighten around my waist, and I scoot even closer to him on his lap.

I hear him groan in the back of his throat. I gasp and pull away for a second, but James doesn't stop, and I can feel him placing small kisses down my neck and along my right shoulder. I move my head back and let out a small moan.

He soon reaches a sweet spot where my shoulder and neck meet. At this, I whimper and pull on his hair a little, earning a little moan from him. He begins to suck hard on that spot, making it feel so much more intense, and my grip on him tightens once again.

"Baby, are you sure about this?" he says as he kisses over that one spot.

I nod my head quickly, and a second later, I feel his teeth graze over my neck as he kisses me one more time before I feel the sharp pain of his teeth sink into my neck.

He holds on tight around my body to keep me from moving, and in another split second, the pain intensifies. I have never felt something like this before.

I grab onto his hair again as he pulls out his canines and licks over the spot, making a shiver run through me again. He kisses his way back up to my mouth and starts kissing me hungrily again before pulling away with a sigh. We both sit there, breathing heavily. A part of me wants to keep going, but I hold myself back.

"You okay, princess?" he asks.

I nod my head. My eyes start to get droopy and heavy.

"Let's lay down for a bit before dinner."

I just nod my head. He leans back on the bed, pulling me with him. I lay on top, straddling him.

"Sweet dreams, princess." He murmurs, kissing the top of my hair. I hear the blankets move around as he covers us before I slowly start to fall asleep.

***

I wake up to see that I was lying on something very warm. Slowly, I realize that I was still on top of James, who is still asleep.

I slowly disentangle myself from him and go to the bathroom. Once I am done brushing my teeth and whatnot, I walk back out to hear him still softly breathing in his sleep. I look at the clock and realize it's around six in the morning. The sun should be coming up soon. I am guessing we slept through dinner last night.

I walk over to the balcony, open the doors, and watch as the sun rises over the horizon. This used to be the best part of my days. The sunrise used to remind me that there were still beautiful things in the world other than the harsh reality that was my life. I watched the sun set in the afternoon and rose every morning when I had the chance. It was my little bit of peace. It was something they never took from me.

A half an hour has gone by, and I hear James stir in bed.

"Grace?" I hear him patting around the bed, and when I turn around, I see him looking around the room for me until he sees me standing on the balcony. "Grace, what are you doing? It's chilly and you are wearing shorts," he mumbles.

He gets up from the bed and walks over to me with the comforter still wrapped around him. When he gets to me, he wraps me up in his arms and looks out with me. Although we are on the sixth floor, looking from the balcony, we can still see basketball hoops and children's toys left in the yard. The driveway is filled with chalk drawings.

This is what my old pack used to look like: a nice house, kids playing with their toys, and everybody getting along. That was just the surface. So many secrets were kept and continue to be kept wherever they are now.

When I look up, I see James looking down at my neck. I quickly bring my hand up to feel some bumps that seem to be in some sort of shape. I forgot to look when I was in the bathroom, so I have no idea what it looks like.

"Want to see it?" James asks with a huge grin on his face. I nod my head, and he quickly scoops me up in his arms. I squeal very loudly at the unexpected gesture and laugh. When we get inside, he sets me down in front of the mirror.

When I turn to look, I see a crescent moon along with the letters JC below them. The moon and the letter show up in a reddish color. It is not a faint red; it's a fire truck red.

I didn't know what I expected it to look like. As a child, when I saw the mark my father made on my mom, I thought it was just a tattoo. Hers was outlined in black with silver shading.

"I am the alpha of the Red Moon Pack, making your mark different from everybody else's. Normal werewolves are all black, but if they are an alpha, the tattoo somewhat resembles the pack they belong to. The JC is my name, James Carter." He finishes while brushing his hand over my mark. When he does that, a small shiver runs through my body, and I unconsciously lean in closer to him.

I hear him chuckle. "It's also a very sensitive area for mates." He leans down and presses his lips to my mark, and I grip the counter tightly and tilt my head back closer to him, exposing my neck more. I also realize I have let out a small moan.

I hear him chuckle and grab onto my waist tightly. When he pulls me backward, I can feel all of him press against me, and that snaps me out of my daze. I stiffen all over, and he must have realized it because he leans back and stares at me through the mirror.

The awkward silence is broken when he spins me around and begins talking again.

"My family will be here shortly for brunch. It will be just a short meal so they can meet you and finally see you. If it gets too overwhelming for you, just let me know. We can head back up here, okay?" He says the last part while looking directly in my eyes.

I nod my head, and we begin to get ready. James showers first so I can have the bathroom to myself after. He walks out in a towel, and I have to mentally talk myself out of going over to him to take the towel off him. Our hormones are going to be crazy until we finally mate, but James promised we wouldn't do anything until I am ready.

"See something you like, princess?" He looks over with a smirk.

I feel my face heat up, and I quickly run into the bathroom while he chuckles behind the door.

Once I finish showering, I get dressed. I choose to wear a simple white spring dress even though it's still fall. I put on a maroon sweater over it and slip on a cute pair of sandals. I look at myself in the mirror and frown. I still don't know how to put on makeup properly, so I skip that and then decide to just comb my hair and let it air dry. It will dry naturally wavy, so I don't have to worry about it too much.

I walk out into the room to see James in some khaki dress pants and a maroon button-up shirt so tight, it makes him look like a bodybuilder. He has the sleeves rolled up to his elbows. The outfit overall is very flattering for him and his muscles.

He clears his throat. "I swear I didn't plan to match with you. I didn't even know what you were going to wear," he says, chuckling. I shrug my shoulders and walk over to him while he is putting his watch on. When I look at his watch, I notice it's about 10:30. Once he is finished, he looks down at me.

"So, you ready to meet the family?"

Chapter 19

When we head downstairs, I can faintly smell muffins and coffee. We get to the bottom floor, and I take a deep breath before we head into the dining room. I see an older couple talking to Dave and Hazel and a girl around my age at the food counter. When she turns around, I see a big baby bump and estimate her to be pregnant for about four months.

One afternoon, Hazel was telling me all about her and Dave and how they got together and how quickly they had Callie. I didn't understand at first, but she gave me an extensive explanation about mating, children, marriage, and other related topics. Apparently, werewolves are only pregnant for six months instead of nine. The alphas can be around five because they are known to be the biggest and strongest, so it only makes sense they grow the fastest.

When the pregnant girl looks up and sees us in the doorway, she squeals and runs over, hugging James while I take a step behind him, unsure of what to do.

"James! It's so nice to see you! It's been so long, and I can't believe I come back and visit to find that you already have a mate! This is just wonderful." She looks over at me. "Hi, I'm Aria, James' younger sister." She smiles at me, and I give her a small smile back.

She doesn't move to hug me, and I think James may have warned his family not to come too close because not a minute later, when the older couple comes over and introduce themselves to his parents, they also stay at least two feet away. Based on her reaction to James, I am guessing she is a hugger, and it must be killing her to rein it in. I reach to at least shake all of their hands, so it's not quite so awkward. I am trying to make progress and not be afraid of everyone so much. Handshakes are a good place to start.

James' parents are William and Isabella. James and William look so much alike that aside from his dad looking noticeably older, they could be brothers. Aria, on the other hand, has a mix of William and Isabella's features.

I look up at James to see him studying me carefully. I smile back up at him and squeeze his hand in mine. When I turn around, his mom is looking at us with a huge smile on her face.

"Alright, let's sit down and eat. Shall we?"

About a half an hour later, everybody is sitting down and eating and drinking coffee and tea. When I only picked one muffin, James takes my plate and begins adding fruits and other items from the table and tells me I have to eat at least half of it. I sighed and reluctantly nodded, knowing I need it.

We make small talk for a bit, and nobody asks me anything other than questions answerable by a yes and a no.

"So Aria, where is your mate? He couldn't make the trip?" James asks.

"No, he had some things to take care of although he still sent me with an army of guards. I sent them all back home after I got here and said I would call when I was ready to go back home." She chuckles.

She looks over at me, and her mate got me curious. Is he an alpha of another pack too? She must have seen the curiosity in my eyes because she began explaining. And I will never forget what came out of her mouth next.

"My mate is an alpha. Our territory is just about an hour or two from here, so I still get to visit here as often as I want." She chuckles, and I give her a small smile. She looks at James and hesitates before continuing. "I don't know if you have ever heard of them before, but he is the alpha of the Silver Crescent pack. His name is Dante Salva."

As soon I hear the name, my throat starts to swell up, and I choke on my food.

I start shaking my head and backing out of the dining room. My heart is pounding like crazy, and my breathing is coming out quickly. It feels as though the walls are caving in on me.

She can't be his mate. He can't be that close. It's not possible. She can't be that close.

I can numbly hear James and Hazel calling my name, but I can't make out what they are saying as I turn and hightail it out of there, looking for the front door. I need to get outside. I need to be farther away. I have to run farther away. She can't get me again.

I find the front door seconds later and bolt out without even hesitating to look and see if James is following me. I don't know if I want him to at this point. He doesn't need this. He deserves better than me.

She is evil and cruel, and who knows what she will do once she finds out I have been alive this whole time. She told them to kill me. She didn't know they kept me.

I keep running, and I make it half way across the huge front lawn and collapse in tears, trying to breathe. I see the familiar black dots in my vision, and I can hear someone come running out the front door.

"Grace! Stop! Grace, what are you doing?" I hear James as he rushes over to my side. I still can't breathe, and I know any second, I am going to pass out.

James grabs me in his arms, sitting on the ground with me, and I whisper right before I pass out, "Don't let her get me."

***

When I start to wake up, all I can notice is the murmurs around me. I am on a bed, but my eyes feel so heavy that I just lay still, listening to the voices around me.

"I don't know, but you can ask her when she wakes up, James. She never mentioned anything to me about any other packs." I hear Hazel's voice.

James mutters a response. I open my eyes only to be met with the lights. I groan and roll over.

"Grace? Are you okay?" I hear the blinds being shut as I feel someone grab my hand. The sparks shooting up my arm tell me it's James.

I open my eyes completely and a second later, I am staring into James chocolate orbs looking down at me. He helps me sit up and then hands me a glass of water. I smile thankfully and drink the whole glass. I look and see Hazel staring at me at the end of the bed. Why is she in James' room?

I am so confused. I think about the last thing I can remember. I remember waking up this morning and getting dressed then meeting James' parent and his sister. His sister!

I begin to panic and look around.

No. She will find me.

"Grace. Hey, look at me!" James says sternly, lightly grabbing my chin. "Nothing and nobody is going to get you. You are safe with me." He pauses and glances at Hazel. "Grace, we need to know why you freaked out when you heard about Dante. Do you know him? Is he the one who hurt you?"

I quickly shake my head. He didn't hurt me, but he knows the person who did.

"Grace, could you tell us about what happened downstairs?" Hazel quietly asks.

I look up at her as a tear rolls down my cheek. I can't tell them. I can't involve them. They will get hurt.

"Grace, nobody will hurt us. I promise you," James says, and I look over at him questioningly. "I can hear your thoughts. Since I marked you, we can now talk to each other via mind link," he says quietly.

I completely forgot about that. I think he can feel my panic and anger because he quickly grabs my hand.

"I know, baby. I should have told you, but I couldn't. You knew you would have never let me mark you if you knew."

Hell yeah! He doesn't need to be in my head all the time!

"Please, Grace, just tell me. I can help you with whatever it is," he pleads quietly.

Well, if he can read my damn mind, might as well put it to use then. No way am I talking and explaining all of this.

So I just think about it.

I remember when I was four and I had bruises from her pinching me. I remember when I was seven and she slapped me for the first time. I remember all the hurtful words she said to me when I was a child, like how I didn't deserve to be the daughter of the alpha and I shouldn't get to inherit the title. I remember the night of my eighth birthday and her saying there was an extra surprise for me, only to be taken away by four men, whom I later knew as Hunter, Cameron, Kyle, and Evan. They were the four rouges who took me for a walk and promised to bring me back to my parents after. But they didn't to return with me. My full name is Grace Salva, and I am the daughter of the previous Alpha of the Silver Crescent pack.

"Your aunt did this?" He gasps.

I nod at him. *The Silver Crescent pack was my old pack. I have had ten years to think over why she hated me, and I still don't know what I did to her. Dante was my cousin. My sister Adeline, Dante, and I were best friends from the time Adeline could walk. We were the perfect trio. We were more siblings than cousins. We did everything together, which gave my Aunt Molly more than enough time to be mean to me without anybody knowing. She would say we tripped while playing or we were horsing around if my parents ever asked about the bruises. They believed her.*

I could hear a slow growl coming from his chest.

"And Dante never did anything to stop this? He let her do this to you? He got the Alpha title out of it, of course, he didn't stop her!" he mutters to himself, pacing at the end of the bed.

"No, James, he didn't know! He always believed our aunt. That was his mother; why would he have any reason to think she was doing anything to me? He was ten when I was taken. There was no way for him to know. Molly may have been cruel, but she wasn't stupid. Dante and I were closer than her and him, and it must have killed her to see her son get along with me so well when she despised me. She wouldn't have told him because she knows he would have told my parents as soon as he found out," I say all quickly before he could go anywhere.

Hazel only hears my last outburst but probably has put the pieces together and realized Molly was the reason I went missing.

"Grace, if she wanted you gone so bad, why didn't she just have them kill you? Why would they keep you for so long?" Hazel asks. James growls at her for even suggesting my death, but I ignore it

"I don't know," I murmur quietly. "There were so many times I wished they would, but they always told me how fun I was and how they were glad they decided to keep me alive. I think she told them to kill me, but they wanted to keep me for themselves. So they locked me up. They probably thought I would never get away or they would kill me before I could get the chance." Tears are falling my face at the memories of being in that house. James rushes to my side quickly.

"I will never let anyone harm you again. Nobody is going to harm a hair on your head. Ever. Again." He growls and then pulls me into a tight hug. He moves to sit on the bed, and when he pulls me over to him, I sit on his lap and rest my head on his chest. He is squeezing me really tight, and before I can say anything, he relaxes his hold a little bit.

"I am going to be downstairs. I won't say anything until you are ready. I promise," I hear Hazel say. I can hear in her voice that she is upset, and she quickly rushes from the room. I hear the door shuts quietly behind her.

James is rubbing my back while I just listen to his heartbeat. It's so relaxing; I wish I could stay here all day long and never face the outside world again, but I know I will have to sooner or later.

For now, I let myself enjoy the peace and safety that James' arms provide.

Chapter 20

We spent the rest of the afternoon in bed, just holding each other. It is a lot easier talking to James now that he can hear my thoughts. I don't have to speak out loud, and I don't have to talk in front of anyone, I can just tell him.

While we are talking, I realize I was only out for a couple of hours, and it is still Monday. James says this is a good thing because the past couple times I have passed out, I was out for days; the doctor says my mind and body have not recovered from the years I spent as captive. Waking up earlier and earlier each time means my health is improving.

"Do you want to go down for dinner? My family is still here. I can bring dinner up if you want. My mom made her special mac n' cheese," he says with a small smile at the end.

I can go down with you. I'm fine now, I link to him.

He nods his head as he reads my mind. We get up and head downstairs. Once we get there, I smell something familiar, and when we round the corner, I see Aria at the counter with Isabella. William is sitting at the counter talking to a dark-haired man. I can only see a side view of his profile, but that's all I need to see.

I freeze in the doorway because even with a side view, I know who that is.

He still looks like the same little boy I knew, but now, his features have molded him to look like a young 20-year-old man with a 5 o'clock shadow. His height is close to James', and he is built the same though not as buff.

A few seconds later, he must feel someone staring at him because he looks up, and his bright blue eyes meet mine. It takes him a second or two and then realization dawns on his face.

A lot of things happen all at once. There is a blur of Dante walking towards me quickly, James throwing me behind him, and a lot of shouting and yelling. Dante is shouting asking if it's really me, why am I here, if they are the ones that took me, and why hasn't he seen me before. James steps in front of me. William holds Dante back while he and James are shouting at each other across the kitchen.

"Stop!" I say it firmly enough so everybody in the room can hear me. Everyone gasps mainly because his family has never heard me talk. They didn't think I could or would.

I step out from behind James, and he grabs my hand.

"James, he won't do anything. Please let me go," I say. He releases my hand, but as I walk closer to Dante, I notice James staying less than 2 feet behind me the entire time.

When I get to Dante, William releases him. We just stare at each other for a couple of seconds.

"Is it really you, Gray?" he asks, using the nickname he used to call me when we were little. I slowly nod my head while tears run down my face.

In an instant, he pulls me into a hug, and I hug him back while crying into his chest. He strokes my hair and whispers how everything will be alright, and how happy he is that I am alive. Minutes later, we pull apart, and James hands me a tissue, and we all move to the living room to talk.

"I'm sorry I didn't tell anybody I was coming. When the guards came back and said Aria sent them home, I finished up my work for the day and decided to come because I felt bad she was alone. I had no idea what was going on. We hadn't talked all day." Dante explains in a rush.

I just nod my head and look at James, begging for him to explain because I am starting to feel overwhelmed and anxious.

Sweetheart, you could have just told me in your mind link. I can still hear you, he says in my head.

Crap! I forgot about that. He grabs my hand. Everyone takes their seats around the living room. James takes a deep breath once everyone is settled before he begins talking.

"There are some things you should know, Dante. We didn't know of Grace being from your pack until today. In case you can't tell, she is my mate, and I only found her a short time ago. In fact, there was an incident earlier today that brought all of this up." James takes a deep breath again. "But before I go into all of that with you, I have a couple of questions," he says, looking directly at Dante.

Dante nods his head. "Anything."

"How long did your pack and family look for Grace?" James questions.

"We didn't realize until the next morning that Grace was gone. Nobody saw her that night, and when her mom went to wake her up that morning, she wasn't there. We searched the entire pack house and the whole territory, every nook and cranny, under every rock. We even considered that she might have climbed a tree or something and had gotten stuck. There were no rogue problems at the time, so nobody took that into consideration at first. Once we realized someone had probably taken her, we sent out search parties all over the country. We even sent some men here because you are the closest pack to us on the east coast. Grace's dad talked to your dad." Dante looks over, and William nods his head.

"I remember. Grace's dad was frantic, I told him I didn't know anything, but we had chased rogues out and through the south side of our territory in the early morning. Leo went chasing after them, but he could never find them, and that's the last I heard of it." William finishes, looking at me sadly.

"Yeah, they sent out search parties everywhere. They tried for weeks to find anything, a scent, something you may have dropped. Anything." He pauses, looking from James to me. "We searched for five years before it was called off. We assumed by that time that whoever had taken you had killed you. There was a funeral, and even though we didn't have your body or anything, there is still a headstone with your name on it in the pack cemetery." Dante finishes while looking down at his hands.

At the end of the story, I look at James,

Ask him if my family is still alive and what happened to Adeline. Please, I ask, giving him a small smile.

He squeezes my hand and looks back to Dante.

"Dante, what about Grace's family? Are her parents okay? And Adeline? What happened to them?"

Dante looks up at James and me and back to James with curiosity in his eyes. Probably wondering why I haven't said a word.

"Her family was distraught after she left. Adeline was six at the time. She didn't understand why Grace wasn't coming home and wondered daily where she was. They are all still alive today, but there is somewhat a rift between Adeline and her parents. She realized after a couple of weeks that you were missing, nobody could find you, and you probably weren't coming back. Then, a year or so after we stopped looking, she became a lot more distant. She doesn't really have many friends at home, and every couple months, when she hears anything about rogues, she goes looking for them, convinced that they took you. I usually send people with her because she practically has a death wish going out like that, but she still hasn't given up and completely believes you were out there somewhere," he says the last part while looking at me. I see him hesitate before he continues. "She was convinced she would know if you were dead."

I have tears brimming in my eyes. Even though I had spent countless nights praying that my family wasn't wasting their lives looking for me, it was somewhat comforting to know that at least one person hadn't given up hope when everybody else had a grave for me already.

I am not mad at them for any of it. They had to move on sometime. It just kind of stings knowing for the last five years of being there that only Adeline was looking for me.

"Grace, I just want you to know that whatever happened, I am really sorry. I should have kept looking for you when I got old enough. I should have insisted on continuing to look for you. We could have found you. Were you here the whole time?" Dante asks, looking from me to James.

I shake my head no and look at James. *Can you please explain? I don't think I could handle it.* I lean my head on his shoulder. He nods, kissing my forehead, and looks to Dante.

"When I found Grace, it was a little over three weeks ago in the woods. She was beaten up, very malnourished, and badly hurt. She was very scared at first, and it took some time for her to open up as much as she has so far. She didn't talk for the majority of the time she has been here. She chose not to and stopped speaking years ago." He glances at me then back to Dante. "You need to understand before I tell you what happened, that if you think at any point you will lose your temper or anything, you need to walk out of the room. Grace still gets scared fairly easily, and I don't need you snapping and having her caught in the crossfire of your wolf." He stares Dante down until Dante finally nods in agreement.,

"I will keep as calm as I can. I promise I would never do anything to hurt Gray." He looks at me, and I give him a small smile.

"Okay, good. So I'll just start at the beginning I guess." He sighs loudly, and I squeeze his hand for encouragement. "Grace was taken by rogues. I'm sure you guessed as much. She was kept in a small five by five cell and had been there for the past ten years. They… they beat her constantly and tortured her for years. She was cut and beat when she didn't listen, and she has the scars to prove it." He growls slightly, and I can see his eyes turning black. Quickly, I intertwine my fingers with his and rubs his arm with my free hand, leaning into him and trying to calm him down.

James looks down at me and tries to smile, which looks more like a grimace before he continues. "She wasn't allowed more than one or two meals a week, and for a human, she would have died, but since she is a werewolf, she made it. The downside to her wolf working so hard to keep her alive was that she couldn't shift until the night she got away. She can't talk to her wolf like the rest of us can. I talked to my wolf about this after I marked her," he peers down at me.

I am confused, he never told me about this...

"He can feel her wolf, she is there, but she is dormant. She won't talk or come out except when Grace shifts. And they still can't communicate. I don't know if she will ever have her wolf come out and we haven't had her shift since we first saw her. Dr. Richards is concerned if she shifts too early before her body is ready, it could kill her. The first time she transformed was a fluke; she didn't mean to do it. She had a lot of adrenaline going in her system to keep her going. But shortly after we found her, she passed out and was out for almost a week. But what I do know is what they did to her while she was there, was so bad that her wolf is hiding. It doesn't want to face anything, and it's dormant in the back of her mind."

I never even thought about my wolf. I never knew you could talk to them. I just thought they were there.

"Grace also isn't completely familiar with everything about being a werewolf, but we are slowly catching her up to speed." James looks at me and kisses the top of my head and moves his arm around my waist.

"When you say they hurt and tortured her, what did they do?" Dante asks while gritting his teeth, looking down.

James looks at me hesitantly, and I nod at him. We might as well get it all out now. Not everyone in our friend group knows either. We just haven't talked about it in detail.

"They beat her, cut her, they constantly taunted her, the-they... uh... they raped her," he says the last part and his voice breaks, and I see tears in his eyes as they turn black. He is slightly shaking, and I lean my head on his shoulder. When I look back up at Dante, he is shaking, and you can practically feel the anger rolling off him in waves. I get nervous, and James follows my gaze.

When Dante looks up, his eyes are pitch black, and I become terrified.

"I should have been there!" He stands up quickly and starts pacing right in front of the couch. Aria is leaning back with her hands over her stomach. If he loses his control, she will be right in his line of fire.

"Dante, please calm down. Baby, she is right here. She is alive. Just breathe." Aria tries soothing him, but he doesn't seem to hear or listen to her. I start panicking. If his mate can't calm him down, what can the rest of us do?

"Dante, you either need to calm down or take it outside. If you shift, you will hurt Aria and your baby. You don't want that." Hazel's soothing voice tries reasoning with him. He looks at Aria who is shaking on the couch before storming out the front door.

I didn't realize I was shaking too until James lifts me into his lap.

"Grace, look at me. Are you okay?" I slowly nod my head and lean in, so my face is pressed against his chest. It's at times like this when I am glad that he is bigger than me. I feel so safe.

James just rests his chin on the top of my head and rubs my back while telling me everything is going to be okay. I take a minute to breathe and take everything in from the past 24 hours. I look up to see Aria slightly upset with James' parents trying to soothe her. She must be upset to see Dante so distraught. If it were James, I know I would be, and I would want to comfort him.

I walk over to her and squat in front of her. "Are you okay?" I ask quietly.

She laughs although you can tell it's forced

"I hear about what you have been through the past ten years, and you ask if I am okay? Shouldn't I be asking you that?" She takes a deep breath. "I can't believe everything that happened. Dante talked about you, you know. He said he had a cousin that he loved. Although he told me he was pretty sure you were dead, I always wondered if you were out there somewhere." She takes a second and looks at her hands. "Don't take that the wrong way. I just think it was easier for them to believe that you were dead rather than out there, suffering somewhere, alone and unhappy. I mean your whole family was distraught for a long time though Adeline struggles the most."

She looks up at me, and I nod my head. "I don't blame them. I never wanted them wasting their lives looking for me. I was gone, and to be honest, I thought they stopped looking after a month or so. I can't believe Adeline is still looking for me. What is she like now?" I ask curiously.

"Well, she is fiercely independent. She doesn't let people get too close, and she completely skipped over teenage years. I think she matured quickly after everything that had happened. I worry about her because she doesn't get close or let anyone in. After her teen years, she stopped talking to your parents altogether. She moved into the pack house where the other teenagers live. She will have dinner with your parents if your mom asks, though. Your parents are doing all they can to be with her, but I think she blames them for what happened. She would never say it, but she blames them for not protecting you." Aria finishes, looking down.

"I never wanted that for her. I was hoping they would all lead as close to a normal life as they could," I say quietly.

"I know, and your parents try, but it is really hard. They have gotten better, and I have tried to get closer to Adeline. She lets me in sometimes but not often. I have only been there two years, though. I wasn't there when everything happened, so I can't understand what everyone feels. The whole pack feels it. You were supposed to be their first female alpha. They were all so distraught. The guards Dante sends out every time Adeline goes looking for you are usually the same people every time. The first time she left alone, some of the older guards volunteered to go because they remember you and they hope to find you too someday."

I nod at her. Just thinking about everyone who had continued to look for me makes me feel a little better.

"So how did you and Dante meet?" I ask, trying to change the subject. I sit, crossed legged, on the floor in front of her with William and Isabella looking at me like I have three heads.

They are probably surprised I am engaging in conversation. It is taking a lot of effort for me to speak right now, and it's slightly uncomfortable, but I know Aria needs the distraction.

She chuckles slightly before she starts talking. "Well, I was traveling with James, actually. This was two years ago, and I was tired of being home. It was summer break, and I didn't want to hang around the pack house, so for three weeks, James and I went traveling around the US. One of the last stops on the way home was the Silver Crescent pack. We had heard that the alpha's nephew had taken over and since we had an existing treaty, James wanted to talk to Dante in person. So, when we got there, I could smell something before we even walked in the door. I walked into the house not even waiting for James, and that's when I ran into Dante, who also seemed to be walking around confused. We realized right then and there that we were mates." She glanced at James. "At first, James was very against it. I was sixteen and still in high school, and he didn't want me to leave. He knew he would miss me." She teased.

"You were young! You are my baby sister. I wanted you to wait until you were 18!" James says in defense

"James, that means I wouldn't have been there until about six months ago, I would have had to wait two years knowing my mate was so far away! That's ridiculous." She rolls her eyes and then looks at me. "He insisted I go home and talk to our parents because it wasn't his decision to make. When we got home the next day, I talked to my parents. Dante said he refused to be so far away from me and ended up following us back to the pack. My parents said it was fine as long as I graduated high school, so I moved in the next weekend and went to school with all of his friends and pack mates. We have been together ever since and got married as soon as I turned eighteen. Not all werewolves get married, but we wanted to be connected and make it official in every way, human and werewolf." She ends her story with a smile.

Chapter 21

After talking a little while, we move to the kitchen to eat the dinner that was abandoned an hour before. Throughout dinner, there was a small talk and Aria catching her family up with recent events back at her pack.

Her pack that used to be my pack.

The whole conversation when I was talking to Aria was about my sister. And I thought about what it would be like when I go back. I know I will have to eventually, but seeing that place and facing my family after everything that had happened seems too daunting right now. I know I can't wait forever now that Dante and Aria have seen me, but I don't know how I am going to handle it.

James must have noticed my sullen mood because the whole dinner, when all I was thinking about was my family and what it would be like to see them again, he was always holding my hand or had his arm around me, rubbing his thumb in small circles. I blocked him out so he couldn't hear my exact thoughts, but he probably guessed. Having him next to me was comforting, but nothing could get my mind off the fact that my family was out there, thinking I was dead.

Aria told me they went and put fresh flowers on my grave every Sunday. My parents grieved while my sister hunted. The thought perplexed me. My sister had to be eleven when she figured everything out, and they stopped looking for me. How would she have gone hunting for rogues at eleven? Even with the extra men, she has to be pretty skilled or she would have gotten herself killed a long time ago.

The thought saddens me. My sister never got a proper childhood. She probably spent the half of it training and looking for me. She needs to get her life back. And the only way to do that is to let her know I am alive, and that she doesn't have to look for me anymore. She won't have to waste her weekends out on trips. She can spend them with her friends or start to make new friends.

When James clears his throat, I look up from my now melted bowl of ice cream and realize we are the only ones in the kitchen.

"Grace, everybody went to their rooms. Dante will come back when he cools down. Aria made sure that he won't contact your family until you want him to. Do you want to go to bed?" he asks while tucking a strand of hair behind my ear.

I nod and stand up, grabbing my bowl of ice cream. James grabs the bowl from my hand, puts it in the sink, and comes back to grab my hand. We head up the stairs, and I start yawning.

Wow, I didn't know I was so tired. Exhaustion hits me, and the trip up the stairs feel like we are climbing Mount Everest.

James notices and turns around, picking me up and carrying me bridal style all the way up six flights of stairs and into our room.

Our room. I like the sound of it. Silently, I smile to myself. I am starting to think of us as an actual couple. The more I think about it, the more I can't picture myself with anyone else. James is perfect in every way, and I never want to be apart from him again.

I think I love him.

He quickly places me on the ground, and I walk over to our closet, grabbing a pair of cotton shorts and a long sleeve shirt.

I change quickly in the walk-in closet, and when I walk out, James is already in bed in his basketball shorts, laying on his back with his arms folded behind his head.

He looks up at me and motions for me to come to bed. I shut the light off and tuck myself under one of his arms like I did the first couple nights we slept together. I haven't slept like this in a while, and with all the talk about what happened, I need the feeling of safety to sleep tonight.

And that's exactly what James gives me.

***

The next morning, I wake up and James isn't in bed. I frantically look around until I hear the bathroom door open and he walks out in a towel and nothing else.

Just one look at him, half naked with perfectly toned abs and bulging arm muscles, has me thinking very dirty thoughts of what it would be like if we fully mated right now.

When I look up to his face, I see him smirking at me.

"You like it, babe? It's all yours."

I squeak and bury my head under the blankets, embarrassed.

He chuckles, and I feel him come and sit on the bed.

"Hey, I have to talk to you." He pulls the covers away from my face. "Dante came back last night. He is downstairs, and everybody is making breakfast right now," he says while brushing a strand of my hair behind my ear. "Do you want to go down and talk to everyone?"

I nod and get up. I quickly pick out an outfit and walk into the bathroom. I jump in the shower and take my time before getting out. I know that everyone will naturally be asking me when I will go home. But I honestly don't know what to tell them. I still don't know what to do or what to say. I don't think I'm ready yet.

When I walk out of the bathroom, James is on the bed looking at something on his phone. Since I was taken in 2007, I'm not really up to date with the new technology, but I am slowly getting there.

"Ready?" he asks as he gets up. Nodding my head, I walk over to the door, and right before we walk out, I grab his hand in mine and stop him. He turns around and looks at me questioningly while interlacing our fingers.

I lean up and put my other hand on his shoulder to pull myself up and kiss him on the cheek.

"Thank you," I whisper and smile up at him.

"For what?" he questions, obviously still confused although he now has a smile on his face.

"For everything; for helping me when I was hurt; for being patient; for being with me despite the fact that I can't be the perfect mate for you…" I trail off at the end while looking down, ashamed. That is my biggest regret.

I can't give James everything he needs. He needs a strong mate, someone who can help him lead his pack, someone fearless, strong, and brave. Someone who is pretty and isn't broken or ruined. Someone better than me.

"Grace Salva, don't you dare for one second think you are not the perfect mate for me. You are perfect in every way possible. You are so beautiful, so brave, and so unbelievably strong to have gone through terrible things and still be standing here today. In my eyes, you are flawless, and nothing that anybody did to you in the past will change that. They took something from you, and that wasn't your choice. You went through things no person should ever have to go through. But here you are, recovering and finally having a chance at a normal life."

He gently grabs my chin, tilts my head up, and looks directly into my eyes, piercing my mind with his words.

"To me, you are still as innocent as the day you were born, and nothing they did will ever change my opinion of the beautiful, strong woman you have become." He encases my hands in his rather larger hands. Tears are streaming down my face as he continues. "I will always be here for you, Grace. You better get used to that because you are now stuck with me for life." He chuckles at the end, and a small laugh escapes my lips. He wipes away the tears that escaped my eyes with his thumbs and leans down to give me a quick but passionate kiss, showing me he meant every word he just said.

If being with the James for the rest of my life is what I get, I will never have another reason to be unhappy, no matter what happens.

James and I walk downstairs, holding hands after our talk in the doorway. I feel better, but despite James' assurance, I know he would be happier if all of this weren't so difficult. Nobody should have to put up with my drama.

We enter the kitchen and see all of the food being laid out: cinnamon rolls, waffles, fruit, cereal, anything you could possibly want for breakfast.

James makes me a plate. He knows I won't even eat half of it, but he tries anyway. My appetite has gotten better, but sometimes I just can't eat. I've gained some more weight, and my bones are no longer sticking out liked they used to. I think James feel better about that, and I feel stronger and healthier though I know I still have a long way to go. A month can't reverse ten years of food deprivation and malnourishment.

We sit down at the table in our same seats from yesterday, and everyone silently begins eating. I see Dante next to Aria, and I give him a small smile, which he returns before getting a pained look on his face and focusing back on his food.

I hate seeing him beat himself up over this. It's not his fault. It's nobody's fault but hers.

It is silent in the dining room. Even James' parents aren't trying to make small talk. I have a feeling I know the question going through all of their minds, but nobody wants to be the one to ask. Will I go back? Will I let my family know I am alive?

"Grace?" James looks down at me from his seat next to me. *Do you want to tell everybody that you know who set you up with the rogues? Nobody knows but me, baby. I think you should decide what you want to do about it. Your family would probably be very excited to see you alive and well. I know this may not be the best time but, sooner or later, you will have to go back. She needs to be punished for what she did, and you can't let her roam around the pack after what she did. She is a criminal and a danger to the pack. Not to mention Dante can't hide this from your family forever.* He finishes, trying to gauge my reaction.

I nod. *Just wait until after breakfast, then we will tell them everything. I don't want any flying food,* I whisper back to him in my head.

I then turn to everyone. "Can we all talk in the living room after breakfast?" I ask quietly. I hear a chorus of 'yes, that's a good idea,' and 'whatever you would like.'

James leans over and places a small kiss on my cheek before turning back to his food. Everyone continues to eat and starts making small talk.

A half an hour later, after we finish breakfast, we are all finally sitting in the living room. James, Hazel, and I are on one couch while everybody else is scattered throughout the room.

I thought they should all know; they are all my friends now.

James looks over at me. I look down, nervously playing with my hands. I take a deep breath.

"I know you all wonder what I want to do about my family and stuff. But there is something else, something I haven't told anyone but James." I pause as I hear some people take deep breaths, probably preparing for what I am about to tell them.

"I know who is responsible for hiring the rogues to kill me," I say quietly. Chaos ensues in the room. Everybody is wondering why James hasn't gone after them and who the responsible person is.

"Why wouldn't you go after them?" Aria asks quietly.

"Why haven't you gone back? Whoever it is, it's been running around our pack for years! Just think of all of the people he could have hurt," Dante says.

I look down and play with my hands. "It's a she, not a he. And I don't think you're going to like this…" I take a deep breath and take every ounce of strength inside me to tell him the terrible truth. "It was your mom, Dante. It was Aunt Molly."

Again, chaos ensues.

Chapter 22

"How could she do this?!"

"She *will* be punished!"

"We are going there right now!"

I hear a mixture of all of their protests and nasty things that are said about my aunt. The last one came from Dante, and before I know what's going on, I see him get up to leave the room.

"NO! Dante, please wait!" I run after him.

"What, Grace?" He whirls around to look at me, and I take a step back.

I feel James coming up behind me, swiftly placing his hands on my hips, ready to throw me behind him if necessary. I can see the whole plan formulating in his head.

But Dante would never hurt me.

"What?" Dante asks me again. "You have been free for weeks! And you knew this whole time that we are still out there! You knew who did this to you! How can you still be trying to protect her after everything she has done to you? She is my mother, yet I will never forgive her for this! Hell, I can't even forgive myself." He chuckles bitterly.

"But you, you want to stay here, and act like everything is fine now that you are free. Well, it's not, Grace. Nothing is fine at all. You should not forgive my mother. You should be over there, giving her the death sentence right now. And you sure as hell shouldn't be forgiving me. I gave up. The only one in our family who deserves any type of gratitude is Adeline! She is probably out on a hunt right now, looking again for you! How can you condemn her to a life of looking for a sister who is already happy? I can see the toll it is taking on her. Every time she comes back empty handed, a little more of who she is, is chipped away, and she becomes a hardened fighter. She acts like she has no feelings, but she does. I hear her cry every time she comes back empty handed. How can you put her through that?" He stops and takes a deep breath. The room is so silent you could hear a pin drop.

I have tears running down my cheeks. Dante has never been angry with me. Not in the years that we were best friends did he ever raise his voice at me. He is angrier than I've ever seen him. I know he has a point, but I can't face his mother or my family yet.

For them to hear what happened would hurt them. Adeline would probably blame herself still. My mother would be horrified, and it would make my dad turn on his own sister.

"Gray." Dante takes a deep breath. "I know that what happened is awful, and everyone who stopped looking for you is to blame along with my mother and those rogues. But you can't keep walking around this house with James and everyone here and act like you're moving on without dealing with the cause of why you were taken in the first place." He looks around at everyone in the room.

"I think it is great that you have found a home with them. You now have friends, and you can build an actual life here, but you will never be able to move on from what happened until you confront the cause and see your family again. This predicament will always nag you in the back of your mind." With that, he walks out the door and gently shuts it behind him.

Tears are running down my cheeks, and as I turn and look at James, I notice that he looks conflicted.

"Is that what you think too? That I should go back?" I whisper while looking down. James cups the sides of my face while using his thumbs to wipe away my falling tears.

"Baby, you know I would never make you do something you don't want to." He hesitates. "But I think you should take into consideration everything Dante has said. Your family is still out there. Is it fair for them to mourn you while you are alive and building a new life? Don't you want them to be a part of that? Is it fair for Adeline to spend her whole life looking for a sister who is no longer in danger?" He is looking into my eyes, trying to gauge my reaction.

Sobs crawl their way up my throat as I start full on crying.

James pulls me into his chest and rests his chin on my head. I fist my hands into his shirt and cry as he comfortingly rubs my back

It makes me sad because I know the answer.

They deserve to know.

Adeline deserves a normal life.

And Aunt Molly deserves to be punished.

I have to go back.

***

About ten minutes later, I calm myself down enough to pull my face out of James' chest. I notice we are sitting back on the couch where we were before, and everyone has left the room. It's just him and me now.

He is looking down at me, wiping away the tears that have almost soaked his shirt.

"Sorry." I grumble. My voice is hoarse from crying.

"Don't worry about it, baby. Are you okay?" he asks, looking into my eyes. He is trying to determine my mental stability right now.

I nod and lay my head back down on his chest. *Where did everyone go?* I speak in his mind because it feels natural to me now.

"Cole had patrol, and everybody else went to their rooms to give us some privacy. They are all very worried about you." He stops talking for a minute and lifts my chin up to meet his gaze. "You know that they will all support you in whatever you decide, right? They will never judge you or try and force you to do anything. Whatever you decide to do, do it for you and what you think is right, not because you are scared of disappointing us. That would never happen, princess."

I nod my head and take his words in. He already knows me too well. I feel like if I don't go back, they will think I am a coward for not facing my family, and a horrible sister for what Adeline is still going through, but even if they don't think that, I do.

I did something I never thought I would do, I escaped. And now, it's time for me to do the other thing I never thought I would do…

Go home.

***

After sitting on the couch and talking a little more, James tells me that Dante has left to go back to his home. He was never planning on staying more than a couple of days, and he went back to watch his mom, in case I did decide to come home. That way, she will be under his watch all the time.

I can't help but feel that Dante is very disappointed in me for not going home sooner, but I had my reasons. If I had told everybody the truth, they would have insisted on going to the pack right away to tell my family and kill Aunt Molly.

I'm not trying to protect her, but I have been here around a month, and I was—and still am—coping with everything that happened. I didn't want to add the chaos of trying to go home at the same time. I also didn't want my family to see me in the condition that James and the pack found me in. That would have devastated them.

James and I call everyone back to the living room.

"Hi, everybody. Thank you for coming back. Grace, has decided she wants to go back to her pack. We will need a couple of people to come with us, but I understand if any of you want to stay behind. I don't know how long we will be visiting once Grace sees her family. It could be for a couple of weeks." He finishes, looking at Dave and Hazel. They have Callie to think about, and they probably don't or can't be away for that long.

They look at each other and give one nod before Hazel speaks. "We would like to come. Grace is my friend now and my new luna. I want to be there for her." She looks at me and gives me a small smile, which I return.

"We will also be coming." William stands up and looks at us. "Aria is very pregnant, and we would like to accompany her back since Dante is not with her. We would also like to be able to help in any way we can." He finishes, looking down at Isabella.

Isabella nods before looking at me. "You are family now. We will be there for you like you are our own child."

I smile and nod at them, a single tear forming in my eyes.

"I'm coming too," says Cole. "I am supposed to be your guard whenever we are not in the pack or when Alpha James is away. I will be there to protect you in case she would try anything."

I give him a small nod. I haven't given him a chance to be around, and I feel bad, but I haven't gone anywhere or done anything, so he doesn't need to babysit me.

James explained that being the guard of the luna is always an honor. They feel important, and it is their duty to make sure nothing happens to her. Some packs even have multiple guards for their luna.

Any werewolf who loses their mate becomes a mess. They feel empty and broken without them. Some don't make it through a year without their soul mate. James compared it to losing half of yourself since they complete you. The few cases where mates go on is usually when they have kids; they go on for their kids and find a way to live without their other half. Imagine the alpha, the leader of the whole pack, losing his other half. The pack would be in shambles.

Rose and Jackson both insisted on coming because they are both good warriors as well. Unknown to me before, Rose is, apparently, one of the best she-wolf fighters of the pack.

James asked Cassidy, Ethan, Brittany, and Caiden to stay behind and take care of the pack. He said he needed people he trusted, and they are some of the only higher-ranking wolves left to be in charge. Cassidy and Ethan are the third in commands, and since the betas are coming, it falls on them to act as alphas while James is gone.

Emma and Mac are also staying behind because they are in charge of watching Callie while we are away. Hazel and Dave didn't want to put her in harm's way in case anything goes wrong with my Aunt Molly, considering her record with kids isn't that spectacular.

In total, we have ten people coming with us so we will be taking three cars. Cole, James, and I will be riding in one car. Aria will be riding in with their parents while Dave, Hazel, Rose, and Jackson take last car.

Since we do not know how long we will be staying, we told everyone to pack for a week or two worth of clothes.

Later that night, James and I are sitting in our room, both of us silently packing our suitcases. He gave everybody a one-suitcase rule, but the girls can have their purses. I don't have anything of my own besides my clothes which will fit easily.

I finish putting my clothes in my suitcase and look to see it half empty. In reality, this is James' suitcase. I don't have one of those either, and my clothes are still fairly tiny, so they only take up about half of the suitcase along with a pair of flats and sneakers.

I look over to James who has his clothes perfectly folded and filled to the top. He easily zips it up and looks at me to see me staring at him with a blank look on my face.

"What's wrong?" He comes over to me and picks me up so my legs wrap around his waist. His hands hold my legs, and my arms instantly go around his neck, and I just sigh. *I don't have anything besides clothes. I wonder if all of my old stuffed animals and stuff are still with my parents. Maybe they got rid of all of my stuff.* I look at my suitcase, still half empty.

"Do you like stuffed animals?" James asks with a little grin.

I shrug and nod my head. They are just so soft, and some are so big you can cuddle with them.

"Well, I have something I want to give you." He is full blown smiling now. He puts me down, and when we get into his closet, he surprises me with a white box with a picture of a phone on it, two of his sweatshirts, and a fuzzy brown teddy bear.

"First of all, the phone is practical, that's your own phone, and I know when we get there you are going to have a lot of catching up to do with your family. I know we have the mind link, but if one of us is blocking the other out for whatever reason, we have phones to let each other know when we need the other. I'll teach you how to use the basics and other things before we go to bed. The sweatshirts are because it's getting cold and you didn't pack any and I want my scent on you as much as possible for the other wolves to smell.

"Lastly, I had this bear growing up. I called him Buttercup. But when I got to about the first or second grade, my friends told me it wasn't cool for the future alpha to have a stuffed animal. After that, I stopped bringing it with me. I didn't sleep with it because I thought I had to be tough and I didn't need something like a stuffed animal to comfort me." He pauses while handing me the bear. "I want you to have it. I realize now that it doesn't make you tough to be standing on your own." He takes a couple of steps towards me and grabs my face.

"Grace, ever since I have had you by my side, I feel stronger. I feel like a better person. I have become a better alpha. You give me strength, Grace, and I want to be the same for you, whether it's simply by giving you a stuffed animal, or taking you to see your family and being right next to you every step of the way. I want to be your strength, Grace, and I don't want you to think less of yourself for leaning on me when you have to. I would do anything for you. You are my other half and my soul mate, and I love you. I always have and I always will, no matter what we go through together." He finishes by leaning in and placing an innocent kiss on my lips. He then wraps me in a hug, and I hold on to him tightly.

My eyes are watering again, not from sadness but rather from happiness.

I love this man, and I want him to know it. I would love to spend every day of the rest of my life with him, building our life together, whatever that may look like.

"James," I say quietly. He looks down at me. "I love you."

With that, I reach up and grab the back of James' neck and pull him down to meet me half way in a passionate kiss. This isn't like all of the other heated kisses we have had where we are in a frenzy of passion. This is a slow kiss, where our love for each other is being poured into every movement of our bodies and our lips. It's slow and passionate. It embodies everything we would never be able to form into words.

Chapter 23

The next morning, everybody wakes up around eight, and by nine in the morning, we are all packed up and ready to leave. Aria mind linked Dante after our discussion yesterday and told him we would be coming. He didn't tell my family that I was coming. He told them that James will be bringing Aria back with some business to discuss.

In our car, James sits in the back with me and makes sure I buckle my seatbelt while Cole drives. We put one of our suitcases up in the passenger seat along with some snacks. It's roughly an hour or two drive, but James still tries to get me to snack more often because meals are hard. I am closer to a healthy weight for my small stature. Not all the way there, but it's progress.

James puts his arm around me and turns me, so I am leaning into his side with my back to him. He draws small circles on my hip with his thumb. Quiet music is in the background, but I don't pay attention. A couple of minutes later, we get on the highway and closer to seeing my family. My nerves skyrocket.

I wish I could say I slept through the entire car ride or I was singing along to the music and talking with James, instead of spending the entire drive dwelling on the fact that I was about to see the woman who tried to have me killed.

And that's exactly what I did. I spent the first hour worrying about what Aunt Molly is going to do when she sees me again. I spent the second hour wondering what my family is going to do when they see me again.

The car ride doesn't take as long as I would have liked it to, and before I know it, the two hours have flown by and we are pulling into the familiar pack house that I haven't seen in ten years.

"Baby?" I look over to James to see him looking at me, concern written all over his face.

I look out the front window and see everyone talking in groups and looking at our car. I notice Cole has gotten out and is standing next to the car on my side with his arms folded. I feel more comfortable knowing he is there to protect me; it is his job. I haven't given him the opportunity to be my guard. When I get to know him more, I'm sure I will be comfortable around him, and we can be friends.

Now that I think about it, I don't really know anything about Cole besides his rank in the pack and that he is one of the best fighters. Whenever he is there, he is always silent. I want to make an effort to be more comfortable and social with all of our friends when we get back home.

Home. Now I am thinking of James' pack as my pack too.

"Because they are sweetheart," James whispers in my ear while pulling me closer to the side of his body. He must have been listening to my inner rambling. "Are you ready, baby? Your family is right inside. You are so close, and I am going to be here every step of the way." He gives me a small kiss on the cheek while I am back to staring down the front of the house.

"Let's go," I whisper quietly.

James gets out of the car first and gently helps me out, and we walk towards the others. Rose and Hazel send me reassuring smiles, and I try to smile back, but I realize it probably came out as a grimace. I look at both sides and realize James is on one side of Cole and I am on the other. I look over at Cole, and he glances down at me and nods, and I nod back. I need to make more of an effort with him.

I turn and face the front of the house and start walking with the two boys on either side of me while the rest follow us behind. I slowly walk towards my childhood home and my family.

As we walk up to the door, Aria and her parents walk in first, and we follow.

As I am standing in the threshold, the realization of seeing my family again after all those years dawns on me. The thought gives me mixed emotions.

I walk through, and James stands in front of me while Cole stands directly behind me but not close enough to be touching me. James right hand is back on my waist, keeping me pressed into his back. I can feel my heart rate pick up as I smell the familiar scents of my old pack and the pack house.

Tears well in my eyes, but I refuse to let them drop. I fist my hands into James' shirt and press myself-closer into his back. He notices and gives my hip a small reassuring squeeze.

I look to my right and then left, and see the doorways and the stairs. If I remember correctly, the stairs should be straight ahead and curve to the right where it leads you to the balcony of the first floor. The massive dining room should be on the left where it connects to the kitchen, and there is also a door directly to the kitchen to the right of the stairs. A hallway on the right leads to rows of doors to rooms and offices.

I peak around behind James and realize it is all still the same and that everyone from our pack is looking at me with sympathy. I try to pull it together and smile, but I feel really overwhelmed and go back behind James. I take a deep breath and inhale his scent as I hear a bunch of footsteps coming from the kitchen.

"Oh, Aria! It's so nice that you are back! How lovely of your family and friends to visit. Does everyone want to stay for lunch? Some of the ladies and I are cooking a big lunch right now."

As I hear her voice, the tears I tried to stop earlier spill over. I hold my breath so she doesn't hear me behind James.

"Uh, Lilliana there is kind of something we need to talk about. Is Leo or Dante around? Dante said he is here when I linked him," I hear Aria say.

"Yeah, sweetie. They are just in Dante's office, I believe. I just linked Leo when I left the kitchen. They will be here any second." After I registered what she said, I look to the right of the doorway, and there stands my dad right next to Dante. He is staring directly at me.

"N-no," he whispers, taking a step forward with tears in his eyes. "I-it it can't be." He takes another step forward, and I take a small one back. He is my dad, but I can't help it. It's reflex.

"Honey, what are you talking about?" I hear my mom walking closer, and she goes to step next to my dad, but Cole moves in front of me, blocking them from my view and vice versa.

I take deep breaths, trying to calm myself down, but I can feel myself getting worked up. James also moves to stand in front of me, and I can somewhat hear him talking to my parents as I try to breathe.

In. Out. In. Out.

"...where you are. Do not approach her, are we clear? I know how difficult this must be for you both, but you need to trust me. You will scare her if you move too quickly."

I look up at the end of James' speech, and he looks over his shoulder at me.

I nod. He and Cole both take a step or two to the side, and right in front of me are my parents, holding each other with tears in their eyes.

"Grace? Honey, is it really you?" my mom asks, her voice cracking at the end. I slowly nod, wiping the tears that are mercilessly falling down my face.

My mom breaks down into a sob. My dad is standing wordlessly beside her. His arms are around her as tears escape his eyes.

"Hi, Daddy," I whisper. After that, I can't take it anymore. They are my parents; they would never do anything to me. I run into their arms. I feel both of them wrap their arms around me, hugging me tightly.

We sit there in each other's arms. My mom and I are crying, and I can hear my dad holding back his sobs.

"Aw, pumpkin," my dad says after a couple of minutes. "Where have you been?" he whispers the last part. We break the hug and just look at each other.

I look over my shoulder at James, and I see the unshed tears in his eyes. I walk back over to him, and I grab his hand in mine. He uses his other hand to wipe the tears off my face and talks to me in my mind.

Are you okay? Is this too much? he asks while I see the worry in his eyes.

I'm fine right now. Thank you. I smile at him and then turn to face my parents.

"That's a lot to explain, and we will get to it later. Right now, all you need to know is that James is my mate, and he saved me." I finish looking up at James with a smile on my face.

I give his hand a squeeze which he returns while grinning at me. We both turn to look at my parents again. I see everyone off to the left of James are either looking in awe or with tears in their eyes.

I see my dad's eyes switch behind me, and then I hear him yelling.

"NO!"

A sharp pain suddenly comes to my right side.

I take a deep breath in, and the pain spreads to my entire abdomen and up my entire body as I feel myself sway on my feet. I gasp for breath, wondering what's wrong.

I look down to see a knife protruding from my side with a hand attached to it. I look up to see that the hand belongs to none other than my Aunt Molly, with an evil smirk on her face. "You should have stayed gone."

She yanks the knife out, and I faintly hear myself let out a small whimper. I fall to the floor, but before I make an impact, I feel strong arms around me, gently lowering me to the floor.

I look up and see James looking down at me with tears in his eyes. I start to feel light headed and woozy, probably from losing blood. I can hear crashes and doors banging open as I stare up at James

"...baby, Grace! Can you hear me? Stay with me. Come on. Don't close your eyes on me, baby. No! Grace! NO! Stay awake!" That's the last I hear.

I close my eyes and give in to the darkness.

Chapter 24

For the longest time, all I can see is black. I feel like I'm suspended somewhere, lost perhaps. No matter how hard I try, I can't control anything. I can't even feel my own body. I am suspended in a black void of nothingness.

It feels like hours, but probably much shorter than that, before I slowly begin to feel my body. It is like waking up in slow motion when I can't even remember falling asleep in the first place. I slowly start feeling my limbs and what is around them before consciously being aware of the fact that I'm already awake, but my body is still paralyzed in sleep.

Warmth and strength surround my left hand while my right hand is just lying limp by my side.

I again try to move or open my eyes at all, but it only drains the little strength I have inside. So, I just listen and try to understand anything that is going on around me.

I think I heard three distinct muffled voices, and as I focused on them, they became clearer and clearer.

"…don't understand. If she were fine, she would have been up by now. It's been a week!" I hear someone on my left saying. It sounds like a man, and he sounds familiar.

Another male voice to my right answers, "I know, James, but she is stable. That is a good sign. The doctors said it might take time for her body to heal completely. Her body is still not at a werewolf's strength like you or me.

And to top it off, she got stabbed. You have to give her time to heal. I don't even know if she is at a human level in terms of strength and healing."

Are they talking about me? James' name sounds familiar.

James? James... James... James! My mate James who saved me! All of my memories all the way up to the moment I passed out after being stabbed by my aunt, came rushing back.

Now knowing that I had been out a week, I wanted to get up! I don't know where my family is or where my sister is. I never even got to see Adeline. She wasn't there when we arrived. I only had a whole five minutes with my family before Molly came around.

"I know, I just worry so much about what it will be like for her when she has to come back and deal with all of this," James says as he lets out a sigh. I can feel him rubbing his thumb over the back of my hand in a comforting way. This motivates me to try to open my eyes again, and right as I can feel them fluttering, another voice talks.

"And that's why you are her mate, James. She has you and all of us to help her through everything."

I hear James mutter out a, "yeah."

The talking stops. The feminine voice sounds so familiar, but yet not familiar at the same time. I try harder this time. I can feel my eyes flutter again. They open a little bit before a bright light greets me. I close my eyes and move my head to the side and let out a small groan.

"Grace?" I hear James next to me. "Come on, baby. Open your eyes, Grace." He is now standing, and I can feel him closer to me than before. I turn my head to him and open my eyes a bit and blink rapidly, adjusting to the lights before I come to stare into his gorgeous eyes.

I give him a small smile and squeeze his hand a little.

"Aw, baby, I am so glad you are okay." James leans his head into mine so our foreheads are touching. He closes his eyes.

How long have I been here? I ask him in my head.

"A little over a week, princess. Everyone is so worried about you. How do you feel?" He opens his eyes and looks back at me.

"Uh, I'm thirsty," I say out loud with a small smile.

He smiles at me and kisses my forehead. He hands me a cup of water. I look over my right and see Cole standing next to the bed with a shorter brunette. She looks vaguely familiar. She gives me a small smile with tears in her eyes.

I drink the entire cup of water before handing it to Cole. He puts it on the counter, and they all turn to look at me.

"Baby, how do you really feel?" I look over to see James looking worried. I shift slightly in the bed, taking inventory of what hurts and what doesn't. When my torso moves, I suck in a sharp breath of pain.

James holds my hand a little tighter and panics a little more. "What is it, Grace?" he asks, looking frantic.

It's nothing. My body is just sore, and my side hurts when I move it. It's not a big deal really. I'm fine. I try to reassure him in my mind, but he can probably see the pain in my eyes. There is a stranger here, and I'm confused why James would let her into my room.

"Grace, don't lie to me. I know that it hurts more than just a little. You got stabbed with a kitchen knife!" he says exasperatedly. I wince at the memory, and he notices right away. "I'm sorry, baby. Please tell me how it really feels, okay?" he says with a small smile which I return.

"Well, it still hurts a lot," I say in a small voice.

"Okay, I can get the doctor in here and see what she says, okay? I don't want you in pain," he says while turning to Cole.

I look up at James and nods at him as I take a deep breath. I look over to make sure Cole is still here when I notice the girl next to him has a lone tear going down her face.

"I'm sorry, uh… Who are you?" I ask quietly. I guess none of them are planning to introduce her, so I figured I should ask.

"Ah—yeah, Grace, about that, she-uh… This is my mate," Cole says, looking nervous.

"Oh, that's nice," I whisper. If she is Cole's mate, she must be nice, but she looks so familiar.

"Grace here's the thing, my mate is—"

Cole gets cut off as a woman with a white coat come through the room.

"Grace! It's so nice to see you finally awake!"

Dr. Kelly introduces herself then continues to check me, poking and prodding at me while checking all the machines. James holds my hand the entire time. When she goes to check my side, she moves the blanket and the hospital robe I am wearing. I see a bandage with a lot of blood on it. I start to panic, and James puts his hand firmly on my chin, pulling me to face him.

"Just look at me. She had to stitch it, and you aren't healing fast. You don't want to see it, baby." He kisses my forehead, and I close my eyes and take in a deep breath.

I feel her wiping around the cut. It stings a little bit.

James gives my hand a small squeeze. I look up at him to see that he is looking down at me with a small smile on his face.

"Do you know how happy I am to see those gorgeous eyes again?" He tucks a strand of hair behind my ear and runs his finger down my jaw. I get lost in his eyes and try to give him a shy smile back. He whispers sweet things to me as the doctor cleans and bandages my wound. It hurts a little bit, but James is quick to distract me whenever he could tell it hurts.

"Now, you technically could go home tonight. However, I want to keep you here for a couple more hours for observation, preferably overnight, but I know you have a lot of families to see. If I let you go tonight, you have to promise to come back if the stitches open, if you get dizzy, or if the pain in your side gets any worse." She pauses and looks directly at James then back to me. "You have to be very careful. No sudden movements as it might hurt to move around. Get plenty of rest, drink plenty of fluids, and eat every meal and snacks in between if you can. You need to get your strength back up to heal quickly. Understood?"

I nod, and she says a quiet 'okay' then tells me that after dinner tonight, I can go back to my family.

James spends the rest of the day with me. Cole and his mate left when the doctor started cleaning up my wound. His mate looked very upset, and she was crying. I don't think she could handle the sight of blood, but that's fine. I forgot to get her name, but I'm sure I'll see her later.

James has someone bring us lunch, and he eats with me while we watch TV and cuddle. I take a nap after lunch, and James wakes me up around dinner time. He says the doctor said I could go back to my parents, and my mom brought clothes for me while I was sleeping. I am hurt when he says she left after, but he explains she wanted to give me space and she didn't want to see me overwhelmed. She wants to sit with me at dinner and talk.

I really want to talk to them considering I only got about five minutes before everything happened. That's when I remember Molly is probably still in this house. I panic as I stare at the door. Did James tell them? Is she waiting for me at home?

"Hey, calm down. Molly is being held in a cell. I told your parents that she was a part of your kidnapping, but I didn't tell them anything else. I promise she won't get to you again." He kisses my forehead, and I nod, taking a deep breath.

I notice the clothes sitting at my feet, and I look at James. *Can you help me get to the shower?*

I move to get out of bed, and James quickly helps me. Once I am standing on my feet, I can feel the stiffness and pain in my abdomen more intensely. I close my eyes and take a couple of breaths before trying to walk. It's difficult and takes a lot of energy, but I can somewhat move on my own. I can definitely feel the toll it's taking on my body trying to heal itself.

"Baby, can you please just let me help you? I don't want you opening your stitches or hurting yourself. I promise not to do anything just… please… let me help you." He comes over and grabs my hand and wraps his other around my waist on my good side.

I notice the clothes in his hand as we walk towards the shower. He helps me get the hospital robe off and starts the shower while I lean onto the counter, breathing heavily. He pulls down the showerhead, so we aren't getting soaked. The doctor said to try not to get the stitches wet.

He helps me in, and I blush, knowing this is the first time since we met that he has actually seen my whole body naked. When he helped me take a bath when we first met, I got into the water before he could see me, and he didn't really stare with all of the bruises and cuts I had on me. I look away, knowing I don't look too great the second time either.

"Hey, look at me."

I look over to him, standing out of the shower with nothing but his pants on. He is too hot for his own good. I look back to his face, and I can feel my face slowly get red.

"Baby, you are gorgeous, every single part of you, okay? I don't care about the scars or the cut. They don't matter to me. You are flawless, and I would spend every day staring at your gorgeous body if you let me," he says with a smirk at the end. I blush at the thought of James wanting me that way.

James wants me for me.

"Baby, do you mind if I get in with you? I need a shower too. I can keep my boxers on." He looks at me.

I nod my head, closing my eyes. I lean against the wall as I hear him remove his pants.

He gets in, and I lean back against his chest when he wraps his arms around me. He is careful not to touch the cut on my side.

For a few minutes, I enjoy the warmth of the water and James behind me. He wet my hair with the shower head, and we carefully get the rest of my body wet, trying not to wet my side. He grabs the shampoo and starts to wash my hair, then his. He goes to wash my body and puts the shower head facing away from us again.

I quickly feel myself starting to get tired from standing. James goes to wash my legs, and I look down and notice that he did keep his boxers on but there is a noticeable bulge. It is probably taking a lot of self-control to wash me and not do anything. I truthfully appreciate him controlling his wolf. He gets to my thighs and must have seen the scars on the inside of my legs because I look down and his eyes are dark black. He looks up at me.

"They did these too?" He practically growls out.

I just stare at him, hoping he doesn't lash out from anger. I nod and take a step back, pulling my leg gently from his grasp. He looks up, and seeing me scared, I see him take a deep breath as his eyes go back to normal. He stands up towering over me.

"I'm sorry, baby. It's just that every time I see your scars, it reminds me of how shitty of a mate I am. I should have saved you. I'm really sorry." His eyes are watering, but I can't tell if he is crying or if it is the water from the shower. He leans down and hugs me, putting his head on my shoulder.

He is not a shitty mate. He saved me. He took care of me.

"No, you are not. Never say that again please," I say out loud. James is perfect and has helped me so much. I would be dead without him. I hear him growl when he hears my last train of thoughts through the mind connection. I wrap my arms around his torso, and we stand there for a couple of minutes before he rinses both of us off and grabs the towels. He takes off his boxers, and I quickly look away. I hear him chuckling.

"It's okay, Grace. I have a towel on now."

I turn to see a towel wrapped around his waist. He helps me dry off, carefully wiping around my cut and cautiously putting a new bandage on it. Apparently, the doctor filled him in on how often it needed to be changed and how to wrap it securely. Then, he helps me put on my sweater and leggings. We walk back into the room and put on the basketball shorts and t-shirt that I guess Cole brought for him. I intently stare at the wall like it is a fine piece of art as I wait on him

"Okay, you ready? Everyone is making dinner right now. We can go eat with them," he says, pulling me to his side again to help me walk.

Are my parents there? I ask in our minds.

"Yeah, everybody is there. We can talk after dinner, and you can talk to them about everything and what your plans are for Molly and the future."

I nod my head as I remember that I still have my aunt to deal with. I realize I never saw my sister and I have no idea what she looks like now. She was six when I was taken.

Is Adeline around anywhere? I never got to see her. I hope she isn't out hunting or getting herself hurt. I quickly mind link him. I need to know how my sister is.

"Uh… Yeah, she will be there. She is in the kitchen with everyone right now," he says somewhat hesitantly.

Why didn't he say that earlier? I want to see her.

Chapter 25

We walk out of the room and down a maze of hallways before we get back to the main hallway where the incident happened.

"You ready, babe?" James looks down at me worriedly. He has one arm around my waist on my good side, helping me walk. I have an arm around his waist as my other hand holds onto his shirt to keep my balance. My side and abdomen are very sore. I get a little dizzier the more I move, and walking hurts, but I want to see my family and I need to find my sister. The pain will be worth it.

I nod my head, and we walk through another familiar doorway before we enter the kitchen. I look around, and I see everybody there.

"Ah! Grace!" I look over and see Hazel walking towards me with a big smile on her face. She gently wraps her arms around me in half a hug because I am still leaning on James for support. "I am so glad you are okay! We were all very worried!" She pulls back and looks at me.

I give her a small smile and lean my head on James next to me. This is tiring. I need to see Adeline. I see Dave walking over towards Hazel, and he looks at me while he wraps an arm around her waist.

"It's nice to see you awake and well, Luna." He gives me a warm smile, and they go back to the kitchen where I see Rose and Jackson helping cook dinner. They both smile and say 'hi' while still cooking.

I smile back and look around for my parents. They are looking at me from the counter while holding each other, tears evident in their eyes.

"Hi guys," I muttered weakly.

"Oh, my baby." My mom stands up and comes to wrap her arms around me. My dad soon joins in the group hug, and with James' arms gone, they are somewhat supporting me not to lose balance.

We pull back from our group hug and wipe the tears from our eyes as I look around for my cousin and sister. James' arms wrap around me again, supporting me as soon as my parents let go.

I see Dante and Aria sitting at the long kitchen table. They are looking over to us with small smiles while Dante has his arm around Aria. Both of their hands are resting on her baby bump. I look on the other side of the table opposite to them and find Cole and his mate there. They stand up, and he wraps his arm around her while she looks at me nervously, tears pooling in her eyes.

Is she scared of me? I am not an intimidating person and, technically, I will be her luna. I am willing to bet she is a fantastic girl and she will automatically be accepted

"Hey, Luna Grace, I am glad to see you up and walking again." Cole smiles as he gets closer to me, also looking nervous. Seriously? Does he think I will not approve of his mate? All of this is starting to make my head hurt. I nod and lean more into James' hold, growing more tired by the second.

James, you said Adeline is here, I link to him while closing my eyes and taking deep breaths. I just have to stay awake to talk to Adeline.

"Baby, she is here." He looks nervously from me to Cole's mate.

Wait...

Cole's mate... now that I think about it, she looks familiar.

"No," I whisper, tears forming in my eyes. I look back to her to see tears rolling down her face.

As I connect the dots in my mind, I realize Cole's mate is my sister. She is here. She is safe. And she is Cole's mate. She will be coming home with me. I can still be with some of my family.

I start sobbing and put a hand over my mouth before I start breathing heavily.

"Baby? Breathe, you need to breathe." I look up to see James looking down at me worriedly as he becomes blurrier. Black dots cloud my vision and the fatigue I felt minutes before is now multiplied and all I want to do is sleep.

I slowly look back to Adeline as everything becomes blurrier. I need to talk to her and my family!

"No, I just found…" My words trail off as I feel the ground coming closer to me before I am gently lifted into warm arms.

She's okay. That is my last thought before I pass out.

***

I wake up and open my eyes slowly, registering the fact that my head is pounding and my body feels heavy. It feels like I have been running nonstop for days. I look around to see myself back in the hospital room that I was in before.

Crap, how long was I out this time?

I look to the side to see James sleeping in a chair nearby, looking rather uncomfortable. I look over to the couch against the walls to see Cole sleeping with an equally passed out Adeline leaning against him.

I sit there for a couple of minutes, breathing heavily while trying to sit up. I feel a sharp pain on my side. I hiss slightly before slumping against the pillow. I hear someone stirring beside me and look over to see James. He opens his eyes and sees me awake. He stands up and grabs my hands.

"Princess, you're awake! I was so worried about you…" He trails off, tucking a strand of my most likely frizzy hair behind my ear.

How long was I out? I ask him in my mind.

Only a couple of hours. He looks to the side table. It's 3:00 am right now. We both look at Cole and Adeline who are still sleeping.

I just stare at them as they sleep and realize how similar Adeline's features are to her six-year-old self. I should have realized it sooner, but she was so young when I left.

Adeline has forest green eyes, and her long brown hair reaches a couple of inches above her waist. She is petite but much taller than me. She is very lean, and it's noticeable how much she trains. She looks like she can handle herself under any situation that is thrown her way.

Go back to bed, Grace, you need to rest. Adeline will be here when you wake up. When you passed out, she thought it was her fault and has refused to leave the room. She wants to talk soon too, so don't worry, she isn't going anywhere. He grabs my hand in his. I look over to Adeline and Cole and nod in agreement.

Will you sleep with me? I look away towards the wall as a slight blush starts covering my face.

I feel him stand up and place a kiss on my forehead. *Of course, angel.*

I scoot over in the hospital bed, and he slides in. At first, it is hard to squish together due to his massive form, and lying sideways is not comfortable for the healing wound on my side.

I stand up and motion him to lie on the center of the bed. He scoots over and lies on his back. Once he is there, I slowly crawl over to him with his help and eventually get on top of him so that I am laying on my front. Surprisingly, his hard chest is a lot more comfortable than I had anticipated. Our legs somewhat intertwine; my feet reach just below his knees. I grab onto his shirt as he runs his hands through my hair. Before I know it, I am drifting back into a dreamless sleep.

***

The next morning when I wake up, I hear soft murmurs in the room. I still feel James under me like how we were when I fell asleep. I can feel one hand drawing patterns along my back while the other is going through my hair.

I distinctly hear James and Cole whispering. They probably don't want to wake me up, but I need to get up. I raise my head from James' chest and look up at him. My eyes squints, still half-asleep. I see him looking down at me before smiling. I rest my chin on his chest and smile up at him.

"Hey princess. How did you sleep?" he asks, placing a kiss on my forehead.

Good. I answer back in our minds. I hiss when I feel a slight tug on the stitches on my side when I sit up.

"Here, baby, let me help you." I feel James slowly sit up with me in his arms. My legs wrap around his waist as I grab onto his shoulders, trying to make as little movement as possible in my abdomen.

When we sit all the way up, I look up at him and blush, knowing I am sitting pressed against him. He chuckles and kisses my forehead. He looks to my right, and I look over to see Cole sitting straight, looking at us with a small smile on his face. I can see my sister is still here, curled in a ball with her head on Cole's thigh, still sleeping. She may be taller and more muscular than me, but she is still tiny compared to Cole.

I look at her and tears start to form in my eyes just thinking how much I missed her and how hard her life has been because of me. I feel James wipe a stray tear that managed to escape my eye. I look at him, and my lips curve into a small smile as I lean into his chest. He leans against the head of the bed. I close my eyes as more tears fall. I know I have my life back now, and I can move on and create a new life for myself, but everything that had happened will haunt me forever. Knowing the pain that I went through and what my family went through, kills me on the inside.

"Do you want breakfast, baby? You never ate dinner," James whispers in my ear.

I shrug my shoulders. I am not particularly hungry.

"I'll have your parents bring us all food. They are looking forward to finally seeing you awake." He kisses my forehead. His eyes then glaze over, talking to Hazel or Dave in his mind, before he focuses back on me and kisses me.

We sit in silence afterward, not wanting to wake up Adeline. James runs his hand up and down my back, avoiding my side, while I lean my head on his chest, just watching Adeline sleep peacefully. I see Cole rubbing her back as well, and I am happy to know that my sister has found her mate.

After all of the sorrow and trouble that I have brought into her life, I'm glad my return brought her something as well—the person who will make her happy for the rest of her life.

About ten minutes later, I hear a knock on the door. I wince at the tenderness in my side when I turn to see who it is. James easily moves his hands under my bottom and lifts me up like I am a feather. I squeal and he turns me around and places me back down facing the other way. I nuzzle in between his legs with his arms on either side of me. I lean back into his chest, still giggling as my parents walk in.

"Hey there, Gray, you hungry?" My dad pops his head in from behind the door before entering the room. They both carry a couple of trays stacked with food.

I hear a shuffling to my left and see Adeline stirring. Moments later, she opens her eyes and looks around the room before they land on me. "Gray!" She jumps from her mate's lap, earning a slight pout from Cole who rushes towards the bed with her.

I giggle at Cole's face, and he looks over to me and lets out a small huff of air.

Adeline wraps me in a hug and squeezes a little too tight to which James lets out a small growl. She instantly pulls back.

"Oh! I'm so sorry! I didn't hurt you, did I? I'm really sorry. I didn't mean to. I was just so excited to see you awake and well. I know you remember me now, and after all these years, you are finally here! You have no idea how hard I have looked for you! I knew you were still out there somewhere, I just—"

"Addy, breathe." Cole cuts her off. "You are going too fast. She can't even answer you." He comes closer, but when he goes to put an arm around her, I see her slight movement away.

Adeline sits on the bed. I can see the upset look on Cole's face for a split second before he masks it and goes to help my parents with the trays. Adeline smiles sheepishly.

"Sorry, you just have no idea how much I have missed you." Her eyes tear up, and her voice cracks at the end.

I pull away from James a little and wrap my arms around her in a hug. It starts out as a hug until both of us start to cry in each other's arms. I feel James rubbing my back without intervening, giving me my space with my sister.

I feel more pairs of arms wrap around us, and I look up to see our parents hugging us too. I can see that they are also crying. I feel James shuffle behind me, slowly removing himself from the bed. This gives Adeline the room to sit next to me. All four of us continue to hug each other and cry.

We are a family again.

I had spent countless nights alone in my cell just wishing to be able to hold my family for just a minute. Even a second would have been enough. And now that I have it, I don't ever want to leave them again.

Chapter 26

After our hug, we pull back, and my parents sit on the bed next to me. I look and see James standing at the end of the bed next to Cole, both of them looking sad but also very happy if that's even possible.

Adeline has her arm around me, and I lean into her. I'm not ready to let her go yet.

I now notice how much of a problem my height is. Adeline is two years younger than me but half a foot taller than me even though she isn't done growing. Why is that?

"So I would like to know everything you are willing to tell us. Where you were, how you got there, how you escaped…" I look over to Adeline, and she has a pleading look on her face. "Cole didn't want to tell me until you woke up, but I know Aunt Molly is involved, and we all just want to know what happened." She rubs my shoulder as more tears gather in her eyes.

I look over at James somewhat panicked. That is a lot to say.

"There is something you should know…" James trails off, looking at me while my parents and sister look at him confused. I nod my head, and he takes a deep breath, "Grace doesn't speak all that often."

Adeline looks from James to Cole to me. "But why?" she asks.

"It's part of what happened while she was… away," Cole says. "Some things you are going to hear are going to be terrible, and some things you aren't going to want to hear, but if you would like to know everything, James and I can explain as long as Grace is okay with it."

Adeline looks at me. "Do you want us to know everything?"

I think for a second and realize that what they are going to hear may change their perception of the little girl they thought they knew. They will blame themselves, and I don't want them to think of me differently. But I realize they have the right to know where I was. I shouldn't keep them wondering their whole lives what had happened to me while I was gone.

I take a deep breath and nod at James.

"Grace was taken. Your Aunt Molly helped in that. It was actually entirely her fault. I'm not sure why, but she gave Grace to the rogues that have had her for years. She told them to kill Grace, but instead, they kept her and used her... for themselves..." He trails off, clenching his jaw.

Cole starts talking and picks up where James left off.

I stand from the bed and gingerly walk over to James. I hate seeing him getting worked up about all of this. It already happened, and it ruined my life, but I have another chance at a normal life now.

He wraps his arms around me as soon as I am within his reach. I can hear him breathe in my scent as I wrap my arms around his waist.

I can hear Cole telling the rest of the story while my parents cry as they listen. Adeline is crying too in Cole's arms. James growls at certain parts during the whole of Cole's narration. I hold him tighter and rub my hands up and down his back, trying to calm him down.

"The doctors have done many tests since she's back. There are a few things they discovered. One is that she may never get her wolf back. She was stuck in her cell, must have been one that's no more than five feet by five feet. This, in turn, stunted her growth. She should be as tall as you guys, especially because she has alpha blood in her system. If she were human, she might have kept growing and had disfigured limbs and posture in the process, but since she is a werewolf, her werewolf was able to stop her growth prematurely. Even if she does get her wolf someday, it won't be very big if she were to try shifting in her current state."

What if I never shift? Or what if I do and it kills me?

We sit in the hospital room for another half an hour, eating breakfast while my parents and sister ask about anything we left out.

They now know it was Molly's fault, but they still don't understand why. Neither do I, quite frankly. That's something they will have to ask her when they decide what to do with her. My parents told me it is going to be done before the council.

As long as she isn't near me, I don't care what happens to her. James explains that there is a trial held under special circumstances where individual packs don't want to be involved in punishing those who break the laws of their own packs. It happens in extreme cases like murder, kidnapping, and things of those sorts. One person from each pack is selected to be on the council, and they serve for life. If they are sent to prison, they go to another pack's prison to serve their sentence without getting special treatment. If what they did is severe, they can get the death penalty.

The packs usually never have problems like this where they need to bring the issue to the council. Normally, packs take care of minor infractions on their own, but Aunt Molly is a special case. Her crimes would not only be kidnapping but attempted murder and being accomplice to torture and rape.

The doctor comes back in soon after to check up on me. After she is done, she tells me I can leave. She says very sternly this time that I cannot be put under any stress. My body is still healing, and every time something happens, it will just take me longer to heal. If something else happens, she says she will be forced to keep me in until I am completely healed.

***

A couple of days later, I am hanging out with my mom and Adeline while James helps Dante and my dad work, talking with Ethan about everything that has been going on in the pack.

I am still learning and catching up on everything my family has been up to and what their life was like after I left.

"For the most part, I don't remember a lot of the time in between. I was really confused. I thought you left, and for a while, I was really mad at you. When I got older and Mom and Dad explained what happened, I began to train," Adeline says in a low voice.

"I trained all day every day. I asked some of the best pack fighters to help me. They understood why I was doing it. They knew what I was doing before I even told Mom and Dad. The first couple of times, I had to sneak out because Mom and Dad wouldn't let me go and wouldn't tell me anything. I was only eleven at that time. Henry, the best pack fighter at that time, caught me one time. I told him I would go anyway the second I got the chance. He must have seen how serious I was because I didn't have to convince him much more than that. He came with me, and we found two rogues causing trouble in the woods. We followed them and found their hideout. We watched them for a day. We knew they didn't have you. When we got back, Mom and Dad were furious. Dad almost kicked Henry out of the pack. He was the alpha after all. I explained to them that Henry hadn't found me until it was too late and there was nothing he could do without giving us away. Dad gave him a couple of extra shifts that week, and that was that." She finished.

"So, did he always go with you after that?" I asked quietly.

"Yeah. Mom and Dad gave up stopping me after some time. Henry was always with me. He never found his mate and was in his forties, so he dedicated most of his time in training me and coming out with me when we heard things." She pauses and looks at my mom before looking back at me. "When I turned fifteen, we went out a week after as soon as we heard that rogues were disturbing some packs a couple of states over. Henry had started asking a couple of friends to come with us, so there were around six of us. We got there, and there were at least fifteen of them.

"It was the biggest group we had seen by far. Usually, rogues don't hang out in groups of more than four or five. Part of the reason they don't hang out in packs is because they don't like authority or the structural order of packs and following a leader, so to have them all together like that, seemingly getting along, was weird. One of them had smelled us, and they all came for us. We were fending them off fine at first, but they kept coming. Henry gave the order for two of the men to take me away and then the rest would run and follow as soon as we were a safe distance. I was strong, but I was only fifteen, and I was still a small wolf. One of the bigger guys picked me up by the scruff of the neck and took off. I didn't have time to stop him. Between Henry and the two other men who stayed fighting, only one came back. Henry had died fighting." She finished quietly.

I have tears in my eyes, and I feel so bad that she had to go through all of that.

"I'm sorry you lost him," I say while hugging her.

"It's not your fault. He knew what he was getting into. I feel bad, but I never asked him to come. I even told him to stop when I got a little older because I didn't need anyone else risking their life. He looked at me like I was crazy and said, *I feel her loss too. She was supposed to be my alpha, and if we find her, she still could be,* and I never tried to make him stay behind again. Nor did I ever try to stop the other guys from coming with us. They all felt the loss of their future alpha. Dante fills that role now, but for a couple of years, the pack was upset. Dad even asked me if I wanted it, but I refused. It was never my position, and I needed to find you. I could never run the pack right. I was not born to be a leader; I was born to be a pack warrior." She looks proud as she finishes.

A pack warrior is a hard position to obtain, and when she turns eighteen, she will be able to go through the tests and training to be accepted.

"I know you will do great. Can you teach me to fight some day?" I ask.

"Of course. We will do it as soon as you are ready," she tells me and offers a smile after. I look towards my mom who has been sitting with us, watching my sister and me the whole time.

"What about you? What have you and Dad been doing all these years?" I ask my mom.

"Well, we had to continue running the pack. We were the alpha couple. We searched and searched for years. A couple of years ago, we lost all hope. We didn't think we were going to find you." She chokes up a little. "I'm so sorry, sweetie! We thought you were dead. There were no signs of you for almost five years. We couldn't find your scent anywhere or anything to indicate where you could have gone. We couldn't keep asking the pack to search, and they needed closure. We put a headstone in the cemetery and had a funeral even though everyone knew we didn't find a body. The pack mourned. We continued ruling until Dante was old enough to be the new leader. Your father continued training him after the funeral because Adeline didn't want the position. As soon as Dante became of age, he took over. It was a relief really. We couldn't shoulder the burden anymore. Your father took it harder. He said countless times, *How can I lead a pack and expect them to trust me to protect them when I couldn't even protect her.' It tore him apart,* she says quietly.

"What do you guys do now?" I ask hesitantly.

"Well, within the first year of Dante taking over, I knew we could contribute to the pack in other ways. I took over running the pack's orphanage. The girl who ran it before found her mate and started a family of her own. I knew she would never leave those kids, and so I offered to let her stay and work there while I run it instead, so she could take a step back and spend more time with her family. The timing was perfect really, and I work there almost every day. Your father advises Dante and helps with the pack's finances. We have a little home down the road. Adeline doesn't live with us anymore, so it's just the two of us," she says sadly.

I look over at Adeline and see her staring out the window. They have their issues, and I hope, with the knowledge that I am alive, they can rebuild their relationship.

***

I spend time the rest of the week with my family. Usually, I see Adeline separate from my parents. I have tried to get her to talk about it, but she doesn't want to. I also notice that, like that day in the hospital, she does not let Cole get too close to her. Sometimes, I see them sparring outside in the morning, and I can see the joy on Cole's face. But it is short lived because, as soon as they finish, she avoids his touch.

I have been eating most meals, and James has always been feeding me snacks whenever he gets the opportunity like when we watch movies at night before bed, when we go for a walk, or even if we are just all hanging out. I swear he keeps snacks in his pockets all the time. I appreciate him caring so much but sometimes, it's difficult to stomach so much food all at once.

I am starting to look healthier than before, and I have put on some more weight. My wound is healing, slower than I would like it to, but it isn't as sore anymore. I saw the doctor again a couple of days ago, and she said as long as my stitches don't rip before they are ready to fall out, I will heal completely in a couple of weeks.

As I chop vegetable to be grilled for the last time this fall before winter comes, I think about James and me. Doesn't he get sick of me? I mean, he has to take care of me all the time. Is he even attracted to me?

I have the body of a twelve-year-old girl. And even when I can have curves one day, my scars will never go away. He probably would never want to do anything with me until I look like a woman. We kiss, but he never goes further than that.

He is a guy with needs, and eventually, he will want something more than just kissing, but what if he doesn't want that with me? Will he go to someone else?

The thought immediately makes me sad, but I brush it off. If James is happy, I could be happy too whether we're together or not. His happiness is the most important thing for me. But my mood sours eventually at the realization that he is only with me because he has to be.

I hand the chopped vegetables to my mom and watch as they take all the meat out to the huge grill in the back. They have a lot of food to cook.

I am standing in the doorway of the sliding door, leaning my head against the door, silently listening to the chatter around me. They are not expecting much input from me anyways, but still, I pretend like I am focused on what they are saying as I think about James.

I look up as I hear people walking out of the woods. I see Dante, Cole, and James all in gym shorts. They all look like they just shifted back to their human forms after a run. I look at James as he walks towards me, letting my eyes take notes of his gorgeously fit body. A brief smile comes on my face at the thought of how much of a hunk my mate is.

He looks all muscular and fit and beautiful, and I look like a twelve-year-old. The smile then quickly slips right off my face. Mood killer.

"Hey, guys. I just have to grab Grace for a bit. We will be down once the food is ready," James tells everyone as he walks by them. His eyes are dead set on me, with an unreadable expression on his face.

I look at him confused. He carefully picks me up bridal style and walks out of the kitchen. I squeal at his actions as I wonder where we are going. He begins to walk towards the stairs and goes all the way to our room.

As soon as we enter the room, he shuts the door and places me on my feet. He stares down at me somewhat intimidatingly; I can tell from his expression that something is bothering him.

"Grace." He takes a step towards me, causing me to step back and bump into the wall. "Tell me if it gets too much," he says. He crashes his lips onto mine, leaving me no time to be confused at what he just said.

Surprisingly, it only takes me a second before I respond and immediately kiss him back. I wind my arms up around his neck, and he slides his arms around my waist. We both deepen the kiss, and he slides his hands down over my bottom, to my legs, and quickly picks me up. I instantly wrap my legs around his waist, letting out a small squeal on the way.

He takes a small step forward, pinning me between him and the wall. His hands are around my butt as he licks my bottom lip. In our rare make-out sessions since he has found me, I have learned that this means he wants to deepen the kiss. Slowly, I open my mouth as the kiss gets more intense and each of us fights for dominance.

Obviously, he wins, and I let him as he gives my butt a small squeeze. One hand stays on my butt as the other trails up to my lower back and just around the front of me. He moves his hand down and slips it under my shirt to get better access. My heart is pounding because he has never done any of this before. We just usually made out and that was it.

I pull away from the kiss to get air, but that doesn't faze him as he continues kissing down my neck until he gets to my mark. He kisses it, and I can feel heat gathering in my face. I need something more, and this isn't something I have ever felt before.

He gently plays with my chest as he kisses my neck and grabs my butt tighter. I am breathing heavily as I feel him slip his hand out of my shirt and back down to my butt. He picks me up from the wall and starts to walk. He starts kissing me again, and I kiss back with equal need.

Before I know it, I can feel the soft mattress below me, and he lays me down. Although he is on top of me, I barely feel any of his weight. He has his elbows propped on either side of him, probably so he doesn't squish me, and he starts kissing my neck again. One of his hands moves down to firmly grasp my hip, and I begin squirming under him. He is placing kisses and love bites all over my neck and mark again.

The need builds, although I don't know what for, as he gets to my mark again.

"James..." I somewhat moan and whisper aloud. James immediately leans back to look at me.

"What is it, baby?" he asks.

My face gets red when I realize that I actually want him to touch me. I have this strange feeling of needing him to touch me. I look away towards the wall, feeling embarrassed of what I was going to say to him.

"Baby, look at me," he whispers while tilting my chin towards him. "I know what you are going to say, and it's completely normal. You don't need to be embarrassed. I brought you up here because you left your mind link open, and I could hear what you were thinking about in the kitchen. Don't you ever think I am not attracted to you. I am, more than you will ever know."

He trails his thumb over my cheekbone while looking at me with a smile on his face. "I just didn't want to try anything more because I don't want to push you into things you aren't comfortable with. We are taking this at a pace you are comfortable with. You are so beautiful, and I love your body. Every. Single. Part of it," he says, kissing me between each word.

I giggle and nod.

"You just let me know what you are comfortable with and we can go from there, but we need to be able to talk about these things because I do not want you feeling in any way uncomfortable. Ever." He looks at me sternly.

My face heats up thinking about talking about sex with him, but I nod my head.

"Was earlier too much?" He sits up and puts me in his lap, facing him.

I shake my head, wondering why that all felt so good.

"It's because whatever we do physically will be just as pleasurable for you as it is for me," he whispers in my ear. I blush as I realize I forgot again to pull a wall up in my mind. He pulls back and looks at me.

"I'm serious, Grace. I don't think you know much beyond the basics, but you will never feel hurt like you were before. I will never do that to you. And as long as you are comfortable, every time we become physical with each other will feel just as good for you as it does for me." He tucks some of my hair behind my ear.

That sounds so strange to me. The rogues said it was only for them and that I was never supposed to have fun… that it was always meant to hurt.

"That's wrong. Do you trust me?" he asks, looking into my eyes.

I don't even hesitate for a second before nodding my head.

Chapter 27

James slowly leans in while kissing me. He leans me back again, so I am on my back on the bed with him hovering over me, never once breaking the kiss.

Instead of the fiery and intense kiss we have shared before, the kiss is slow, and James is more caring with his movements. The next second, I can feel him moving his hand down to my hip. He grasps the edge of my shirt while deepening the kiss a little more. After a minute or two, he leans back.

"Babe, you can tell me anytime if you don't like what's going on, okay? I'll stop the second you say so." He looks into my eyes like he is willing me to understand that this is on my terms.

I nod my head while biting my lip, getting a little nervous. I'm not sure what's going to happen, but I trust James not to hurt me.

He leans in and kisses me again. His hand goes down to my shirt and gently lifts the shirt up my torso, giving me time to stop him if I want to. We break the kiss as he completely takes off my shirt and runs his hand back down my side and back up again, gently grabbing my breast.

He trails kisses down my neck and to my mark briefly as I hold back my moan, embarrassed of moaning again. I then feel his hand move down to the top of my leggings. He hesitates at the waistband, waiting to see if I am going to stop him.

I trust him not to hurt me.

He slowly slides them off my legs. And with that, James shows me what I've been missing.

***

The rush of euphoria fades and I sink back into the pillows. James comes back up to lay beside me, dragging the blankets up with him, and covers me. He props himself up on one elbow and looks down at me as his other hand slowly tucks my wild hair out of my face.

I sit there breathing heavily, not knowing what to say. *What was that? Does that always happen?*

"Yes, princess. It can happen every time we do stuff if you would like it to." He leans in and kisses my forehead.

I blush, realizing I was moaning loudly just now. I am so embarrassed, I can feel my face heat up. I look away from him, trying to hide my blush. His hand gently goes under my chin. He then turns my head to face him.

"Babe, you have nothing to be embarrassed about. Everything that just happened is completely normal. You can ask me any questions you would like, and if you don't want to talk to me, I'm sure you can talk to your mom. You need to understand that what happened with those rogues wasn't okay. It wasn't normal, and that's not how things are supposed to be between two people. People pleasure each other all the time. It's okay." I look over at him as he finishes and gives him a small smile.

A thought suddenly crosses my mind. *What would it be like to touch him? Would he want me to?*

I used to not do anything. The rogues used to tell me to sit still and not move.

"Do... do you want me to…?" I stutter out, nervous of what I would say.

He kisses my forehead and brings me to him with my head tucked into the space under his chin.

"No, baby. I'm fine. Today was about you, not me." He kisses my forehead, and I lean into him. I can feel him pressed into the lower part of me.

"Are you sure?" I ask, rubbing slightly against him to let him know that I know he is aroused. I feel bad he is left like that.

"Yes, baby. Today was all about you. We will have plenty of other times for plenty of other things. Why don't you ask Hazel or your mom about other things you aren't comfortable asking me. And when you are finally comfortable, we can do those other things, alright?" He pulls back to look at me.

I nod my head and lean back into his chest, wrapping my arms around his torso and pulling myself closer to him.

Suddenly, I realize I am still naked and we will be having lunch soon.

***

We lay there for a couple more minutes until James says his parents are mind linking him that lunch is finally ready.

I get dressed while James says he needs to take a cold shower to calm himself down although I don't know what he means. I just ignore it and go to where our bags are. We have been here for so long that I have worn almost everything though my mom always offers to do our laundry. I think it's just comforting to be able to do something now that I am back here.

Our clothes are folded on the shelf next to our bags in neat piles. I go through the piles and grab new leggings and a sweater. I am kind of cold again and being naked didn't help. I have goose bumps, so I decide to put on one of James' sweatshirts. I'm sure he won't mind.

I pull it over my head, and it reaches just above my knees. I see this and just shrug my shoulders. It's comfortable. I hear the door open, and James walks over in a towel. I blush but hug him when he gets close enough. He is pretty warm despite his weird cold shower.

"Hi, baby. Nice sweatshirt." He pulls back and looks at how big it is for me and chuckles a little bit. I blush and look down at it. It could literally be a dress. "I'm just going to put some clothes on then we can join them downstairs, okay?"

I nod my and sit on the bed. James picks up some basketball shorts and a shirt. I watch as he suddenly drops the towel, and I squeak and cover my eyes before I can see anything. I hear him chuckle again. A minute later, he tells me he is dressed.

We walk downstairs, and I see Hazel. She gives me a smirk like she knows what we just did. I blush and quickly walk to my seat.

Lunch passes quickly, and so does the afternoon. After dinner, my parents say they want to have a bonfire with the pack.

Besides Dante and Adeline, I didn't really have a lot of friends. A lot of kids were too intimidated because I was the alpha's daughter. The kids were friendly but kept to themselves. It will be interesting to see the rest of the pack. They have probably already heard that I've come back home.

"Grace, there is something else we need to talk about," my mom says hesitantly.

I look between her and James. They are obviously thinking the same thing. James looks at me with a hesitant look before he begins speaking.

"Honey, your parents want to know what you would like to do about your Aunt Molly. We have been here for almost two weeks now, and next Sunday, we have to go back to our pack." He looks at me, judging my reaction.

I thought The Council takes care of that... I trail off in our minds, leaning into him more.

"Yes, baby, they do. But we're wondering if you want to talk to her or even ask her why before we leave. Closure might help you finally move on and be done with this part of your life," he speaks softer at the last part.

I mull over in my head what he just said. It would be nice to know what caused her to do all of those terrible things she did. But do I want to come face to face with the woman who is responsible for the last ten years of my torture? The woman who just recently stabbed me?

I think a little more and come to a decision.

I'll talk to her. I look up at James.

He nods and kisses my forehead. He relays the message to my parents.

Chapter 28

A little while after our conversation, James and I go back to our room to get ready for the campfire. James puts on pants and a sweatshirt. He gives me a slightly smaller sweatshirt to put under the big sweatshirt. My immune system sucks, and apparently, I can get sick fairly easily. It has gotten very cold now and will probably start snowing next month.

We grab shoes and walk out and reach the back yard where a huge outdoor fireplace made of stone is surrounded by a total of seven other little fireplaces in every 100 feet. Some of the pack members built this when I was very little so that they could have fires when they wanted and the woods around us wouldn't be in danger of catching fire. It's much better as opposed to just having bonfires on the ground.

There are chairs around every fireplace. I see teenagers around their own fires, families around a couple of the other fires, and adults around the remaining fires. Although they are somewhat split up, people freely walk in between every fire, mingling. Most of the children are in bed. My family and friends are around the biggest fireplace.

James and I walk slowly towards them, and when we get close, he sits in a big chair and pulls me onto his lap.

Memories of campfires in the summer time come rushing back. I was sitting in this exact same chair with Dante and Adeline the weekend before I left. It was mid-November, and it hadn't snowed yet. I asked my parents if we could have a campfire in the back yard with everybody there for my birthday.

We had it on the next weekend because my birthday was in the middle of the week and my parents don't want me to stay up on a school night.

The three of us had taken a picture, making silly faces, and my mom had said she would put it in a frame in my room. Since our stay here, I haven't been to my old room. It is on the top floor with the rest of the alpha rooms. I wonder what they did with my stuff.

My room had been the typical princess room—all decked out in purple. The walls and curtains were purple; my comforter has different patterns in shades of purple. I had a big bed and a desk in the corner. I used it for my homework when I didn't do it with my parents downstairs. I would paint or draw occasionally, so I kept all of my art stuff there too, along the wall at the top of the bed with all of my other drawings. I drew my family and the woods around us. I was eight, so they weren't too great, but they were okay.

I sit there staring at the fire, picturing my room and thinking about all the memories that Dante, Adeline, and I had in that room. We were so close, and we always hung out in there. We preferred my room to theirs since my room was the biggest of the three of us and I had a huge window with a big window seat.

I can feel James trailing his hand up and down my arm. I snuggle myself back further into him. This chair is kind of like an outdoor love seat, so we fit in perfectly. Even if it wasn't, James takes up the chair, and I fit my whole body on his lap comfortably.

I turn around in his lap, so I am straddling him and lay my head on his chest. He moves his hand, softly rubbing my back. *You okay, baby?* He links.

Yeah, just so many memories. I take a deep breath.

I suddenly get an idea. I think about the memory of Dante, Adeline, and I in this chair and share the memory with James through our mind link. I hear him take in a deep breath.

"Did you just do that?" he asks out loud. I look up at him with a small smile. "I didn't know that was something mates could do," he says, confused.

I just shrug my shoulders. I close my eyes and think about another memory. One summer when I was seven, Dante and I discovered a place where there was a waterfall with a small pond that led to a stream. We used to go there all the time. We only found the place because we had been playing at the lake with the pack and the families, and we followed a stream we found at the edge of it. When we followed it back, we found the pond and the waterfall. It was so beautiful.

I showed him memories of the first time Dante and I went in. Adeline was five so she couldn't come with us. The water was warmer than the lake water, so we liked to go swimming there. When Adeline was six and hung out with us more, we showed her the place, and it eventually became the place we would go whenever we needed an escape. We built a rope swing to go into the pond. It was attached to a huge tree at the edge of the pond closer to the falls. Dante had done that because Adeline and I were too scared to climb up the tree to tie the rope.

I showed another memory of us in my room sitting on the window seat. I was trying to draw Dante, but it came out horribly, and we ended up laughing so hard that my parents came in to see what was wrong.

Memory after memory goes through to James as I show him the happiest memories I have with my family before I was taken. I open my eyes to look at James and see a huge grin on his face. I can't help but break into a huge smile.

"That's amazing." He breathes out. I nod and giggle a little bit.

"It's so good to see you smiling and happy. I want to remember those memories forever," he whispers while he brings his hand up to brush his thumb across my cheek.

"Hey, look over here!" I hear someone yell. I look over in time to see a flash. When the flash goes away, I see my mom with a phone in her hands. She smiles at me, and I give her a smile back. I see tears well up in her eyes.

"I need some more pictures of my baby now that she is back." I see a tear spill over, and I get up from James' lap to walk over and hug her. She hugs me back and holds onto me tightly like she thinks I will disappear.

"Want me to take a picture of you guys?" I hear James behind me.

I turn around in time for my mom to hand him the phone. My mom calls over Adeline and my dad. James takes our first family picture since I got back. Several more pictures with the rest of our friends are taken after that. There's with me, Adeline, Cole, and James, and another with Aria and Dante joining us. We even recreate the one of Dante, Adeline, and I in the chair. We take more with all of our friends from our pack.

By the time we settle into our seats again, we probably have close to thirty pictures. Now that I think about it, I hadn't had a single picture since that campfire before I was taken. I think about starting a photo album. I wonder again where my stuff from my old room went. I want those old pictures too. I can hang them in our room back in our pack.

I sit there thinking I about saving to buy a camera of my own. Maybe I'll buy a nice actual camera that takes good pictures, and I can then start a photo album. I'll take pictures of everything. Memories are too important to lose.

I want to capture every memory of my second chance at life.

***

We sit at the fire for another half an hour, and by now, it's around nine. James went to the house to get us both drinks. I am curled up in the big chair by myself when I see Adeline walk over to me. Since I have been back, I feel like we have gotten closer although she still won't talk to me about our parents or Cole.

"Hey, you want to take a walk with me?" she asks, holding out her hand.

I nod and get up from the chair, taking her hand for help. We link arms and begin to walk to the pack house. I wonder where James is and I link him to tell him I am with Adeline, to which he replies 'okay' and that he will be by the fire with Cole.

We walk into the house and up the stairs. We get to the alpha floor, and I begin to get confused as to what we are doing here. We walk down the hallway before we stop in front of a door that I recognize. I look over at Adeline, and she gives me a reassuring smile. I unlink our arms and, with a shaking hand, open the door.

I walk into the room with tears in my eyes. Everything is exactly how I remember it: the purple curtains and walls, the made up bed with the same nice and neat patterned comforter. Even my drawings are still on the wall. My eyes tear up as I look at the very poor drawings of my family and the house. I even see the one with Dante sitting in the window seat. I chuckle out loud at that one before I move over to my desk.

Above the desk are all of the pictures from when I was younger, untouched. I realize the only new thing is the picture in the middle of the desk. It was taken on my birthday. We were sitting by the fire. My mom must have had it framed and put it here after I was taken.

I walk over to the window seat and sit down. I look at the sides and see all of my books still in the built-in shelves in the walls on each side of the window. They are short books because I was small, but some of my favorites are in there, too. I always loved reading. The idea of living hundreds of different lives through the characters in the books always seemed surreal to me.

I can see the bookmarked page in one of the Magic Tree House books. I pick it up and open to the page. James was giving me books like this to try to help me because I really still read at an 8-year-old level, which is quite embarrassing.

I turn around and see Adeline still in the doorway, not coming into the room, studying me carefully.

"Mom and Dad didn't want to get rid of any of your stuff. They always thought that if you did come back one day, you would need this room. They wanted it to stay exactly how you left it. It was the only way I knew they hadn't completely given up hope." She takes a deep breath and looks around before speaking again. "James heard your thoughts earlier and asked Cole if we had any of your old stuff. I talked to Mom and Dad, and they said it's up to you what you want to do with any of this stuff or this room. Technically, this is Aria and Dante's floor since they are the Alpha and Luna, but nobody could bear to get rid of your stuff." She finishes, looking sad.

I look around and realize there is no reason anymore to keep the room the way it is. I am back, and they don't need to keep this and keep walking on egg shells around this room.

"Could I take some of the stuff? Like the pictures and some other stuff? Dante and Aria can use this room. I don't see the reason to keep it this way any longer, and I think it is another step in helping everyone move on from what happened." I look at her. "If there is anything you want to keep in here, you can too. You and I can go through it sometime with Mom and see what we want to keep and what we don't."

She nods her head. "Yeah, I think that's a good idea. We can all do that sometime this week if you want."

I nod and take one last look around the room before walking towards her. We walk out and shut the door.

We make our way back outside with our arms linked and rejoined the rest.

I immediately walk over to my mom and give her a hug. "I love you, Mom," I whisper.

"Baby, I love you too," she says, hugging me back.

After the fire, we all head up to bed. Once James and I get into our room, I go to the bathroom, do my business, and change. I walk out, and James is sitting on the bed in sweat pants and a tank top shirt. We crawl into bed, and before I know it, I am fast asleep.

Chapter 29

The rest of the week passes by uneventfully. My mom wanted to keep all of my drawings and, one day when James was out, he got me my own photo album. I took all of the pictures off the walls and put them in there. I asked my mom for the recent pictures we've taken, but she doesn't know when those will be in available. Perhaps sometime within the next week or so, she told me.

I kept all of the books to help me read a little better. My mom kept all of my old clothes, saying they could be hand me downs for the orphans of the pack.

We haven't really discussed who will be leaving, but it is clear Adeline will be coming with us. She and Cole have been spending time together, but I notice how she hesitates anytime they get too close. I can see her becoming more comfortable opening up to him and talking to him, but physically, she is not affectionate towards him. I can see him holding himself back as well, but it must be really hard for him.

This week, Adeline taught me basic self-defense techniques that don't require too much energy, like how to break out of holds or if an attacker is too close and which vital places to hit. She promised to teach me hand-to-hand fighting when we get back to our pack.

My mom and Adeline also had the talk about the birds and the bees with me. I know how sex works, and they told me how it's supposed to feel and how it was so wrong of the rogues to do what they did. They also told me what James had done and why it felt good and other things people do besides sex. It was embarrassing, to say the least. I asked questions, even the really embarrassing ones, and after that, I felt like I knew a lot more about the subject. I am somewhat comfortable with it although not as comfortable to try any of it—yet.

It's Saturday right now, and we are planning on leaving tomorrow morning. I am going to miss my parents, but I understand if they didn't want to uproot their lives to move a couple of hours away.

"Hey, hun, could you mix all of this into a salad?" my mom asks.

We are making dinner for the family as a kind of goodbye dinner since tonight is our last night. All of the girls are behind the counter cooking. I am assuming James told them about the last incident in the kitchen because they give me minimal tasks like putting the salad together.

Aria is sitting next to me, rubbing her baby bump. Nobody wants her working too hard since it could put stress on the baby.

I grab the ingredients and put the salad together. Once I finish the salad, I grab the different dressings and place them on the table next to the salad. I look over to the kitchen to see that they are placing all of the meat on the trays and the rice and other things in bowls. I go over to grab a bowl from Hazel, who has her hands full, but two large hands beat me to it.

"I got it, princess. Why don't you go sit down?" James suggests. I can feel him right behind me, and I turn around. He gives me a kiss on the cheek and steps to the side so I can pass. I look and see all of the guys have come back and are taking bowls and platters from the women to help.

Cole takes Hazel's other bowl and holds her hand instead, leading her to the table. Dante takes everything out of Aria's hands and tells her not to lift things. Aria is due any day now, and he is getting extremely protective over everything she does. It's kind of cute.

Everything is set at the table, and once everybody sits down, we begin to eat. Everybody makes small talk as we eat. My appetite is somewhat better. James always tells me to eat as much as I think I can. Afterwards, all of the men offer to clean up while the ladies sit around the table and talk, but I am focused on James.

He really has done everything for me. He saved me. He took me back to my family. And he continues to take care of me every day, no matter how difficult it is. He has done so much, and I have never heard him complain once about any of it.

The men are done and are already making jokes in the kitchen. I get up and walk over to James, wrapping my arms around his waist from behind. I bury my head in his back and just try to memorize everything about him—how he feels in my arms, his scent, anything I can cling to.

"Hey, sweetheart. What's going on?" He turns around, looking slightly alarmed. My arms snake back around his waist as I look up at him. He puts his hands on either side of my face and brushes my hair out of my face with his fingertips. I just shrug and lay my forehead on his chest.

"Do you want to go for a walk?" he asks. I nod my head against his chest. We turn for the door, waving bye and telling everyone we will be back soon.

I keep one arm around James as we walk side by side out the door. He wraps his arm around me. Once we get through the door, the sudden chill hits me, and I shiver.

"Hold on, I have a sweatshirt downstairs." James leaves me at the door and walks over to the coat hanger. He gets his sweatshirt out from under some other coats and brings it over to me.

"Here," he says, opening the bottom for me so I can put it on. I slip my head through it and put my arms in the sleeves. The sweatshirt goes all the way down to my knees, and there is no chance at all for me to put my arms all the way through. It is big and warm with my big sweater under it. He pulls my beanie off the hat rack and puts it on my head too as we head out.

We walk around the garden for a little before he starts talking about things. I just nod along, wondering what I would do with this man in my life. I blocked him out when we were in the kitchen because I didn't want him hearing all of this.

I stop walking and face him. He looks down at me, a little concerned. "What's wrong baby?" he asks, cupping my face.

"Nothing," I say, tears forming in my eyes. Not the sad kind but the happy kind, knowing that I get to spend the rest of my life with this man.

"Baby, please," he whispers. He looks so worried with his brow all scrunched up. I reach my hands up and pull them out of my sleeves. With my thumb, I run it along with his brow and give him a small smile.

"I love you." I am smiling so much right now. "I love it when you are so focused on something and your lips purse to one side. When you get concerned, you scrunch your right eye brow. I love it when you are so carefree and you laugh and smile like you don't have a care in the world. I love how you take care of me, even when I don't want you to. You do these little things when you think I'm not paying attention. Like when we sleep and if I'm not pressed against you, you reach out to find me and kiss my forehead before you go back to sleep. Or when you know it's cold out, and I have a jacket, you always grab one for yourself to wear even though you won't get cold, just in case I need it." I pause to take in his smiling face and take a breath before I continue.

"But what I love the most is you as a person. I love the way you take care of your family, how you show you love them. You believe in right and wrong, and you do everything you can to do what is right, not just for yourself, but for everyone. You care for those around you, and it's like second nature to you. You would fight for anybody in the pack or your family, and that is something people look up to you for. You protect them with your life and take care of them when needed. I honestly feel like the luckiest girl in the world to have someone as amazing as you. I just thought you should know that I am completely and one-hundred percent in love with you."

I keep my hands next to his face, pulling him down to kiss him.

That's the most I have spoken in ten years, and I meant every single word of it.

He weaves his arms around my waist and picks me up, spinning me around. I giggle as I bury my head in his shoulder. He places me on the ground, and one of his hands comes up to rest on the side of my face, caressing my cheek with his thumb.

"You have no idea how much you mean to me. I love you so much, baby." He pulls me in for another kiss, this time a slower, more passionate one. We pull apart, and he smiles down at me. I swear his eyes are sparkling right now. His happiness is contagious.

"Can I be totally cliché and say that I would like to dance with you right now?" He is still smiling down at me.

"But I don't know how to dance," I whisper.

"I have an iHome back in my room. I can teach you all kinds of dances, and we can dance around before we go to bed."

"You know how to dance?" I ask, puzzled.

"Yeah, it's a part of being an alpha. You get taught how to dance when you are younger because of all the balls and parties you need to attend. I know a lot of formal dances, actually," he says, looking smug. I just laugh a little.

"Hmmm," I think teasingly as I put a finger on my chin. "I suppose we can."

Chapter 30

We walk through the garden for a little longer before heading to the house. I take off James' sweatshirt inside but keep my hat on because my ears are still a little cold. Once our shoes are next to the door, we walk in to find everybody and say goodnight. Everybody is in the living room, just chatting and hanging out.

"Wait!" I turn to look at James. "Could we hang out with them a little longer? Since we leave tomorrow, I want to be with them a little more," I tell him the last part quietly.

"Of course we can, baby." He kisses the top of my head.

We walk into the living room, and I sit next to my mom, who is next to my dad, on the couch. She puts her arm around me, and they both look over to me.

"I'm going to miss you guys," I whisper, leaning my head on her shoulder.

"What are you talking about, Gray?" My mom looks down at me, confused.

"Well, I know it's only an hour or two drive, and we can visit all the time, but I do have to go back tomorrow with James," I say, a bit confused with her reaction.

"I know that, baby doll, but we are coming with you," she says, smiling down at me. I look over to my dad who is also smiling.

"What?" I murmur, confused.

"We just got our baby back. We aren't leaving you! With your sister leaving with Cole too and with Dante being the alpha, there is nothing left for us here, baby. I don't imagine you and James want two packs to take care of. Dante is taking care of the pack and doing a fantastic job. He doesn't need us here. James says if we want to join his pack, we are more than welcome to." She explains.

I look from her to my dad and finally to James, who is still standing in the doorway. He gives me a small smile. I jump up from the couch and run over to him. I leap up into his arms.

"Thank you so much," I say in his ear.

"Anything for you, baby," he says back, kissing my cheek.

I walk back over to the couch with James in tow behind me. We spend the rest of the night chatting with everybody.

***

The next morning, I wake up and begin to pack my bags. James is packing his next to me.

"Babe?" he asks, facing me.

I look over at him and raise my eyebrows.

"I will never make you do anything, but I think you should go see your aunt before we leave. You kept putting it off all week, and I know it scares you, but I think it could be good for you. The Council will decide her fate, and honestly, anything less than the death penalty will shock everyone. This could be your last chance to ask her anything you want to ask her," he says, looking at me, waiting for my reaction.

He grabs my hand as he sits down on the bed, pulling me between his legs. "I just think it would benefit you to get closure, to hear an answer one way or another. I think it's your right to know why she did it, find out if she is just a really terrible person that everyone believes she is."

He stares at me while I think it over. I nod my head and turn back to my bag.

"Wait, do you actually want to?" he asks in disbelief.

I zip up my bag and walk back over to him. "If you believe it can help me move on, then I trust you. Will you be there?" I ask quietly.

"Of course. I'll be there whole time. She will be in a cell so she can't get near you, I promise," he says, pulling me down onto his lap and giving me a quick kiss.

"Okay," I say.

"I'm so proud of you, babe. I'm going to check on everyone to make sure everything is all set then I'll come finish packing and grab the bags. Once the cars are all loaded, we can see your aunt and leave right after that. Do you want to come downstairs?" he asks, standing up.

"No, I can finish packing your bag for you. I want a couple of minutes alone to think and prepare before I talk to Molly... if that's okay." I add the last part in case he wanted me to go now.

"Whatever you want to do is okay, babe. You don't have to ask." He kisses my forehead and walks to the door. He stops and turns around, looking at me. "I love you," he says with a smile.

"I love you too," I say back.

He walks out the door, and I gather the rest of his clothes, pack his bag, and zip it shut.

I walk over to the balcony, thinking about my aunt. Of course, I always wanted to know why she did what she did, but I was always scared of her answer. I know she hated me as a child, but was it enough to want me killed? What did I ever do to her?

I hear a thump behind me, and I turn around to see a strange man in the doorway of the balcony. He walks over to me, and that's when I see the cloth in his hand. I am getting a really bad feeling about this. I quickly look around for an exit. I start to panic and then realize I have two choices: jump off the balcony or see what this man is going to do.

By the time I look back up, he is right in front of me. I feel his hand behind my head as his other hand covers my mouth with a cloth. When I inhale, I realize the cloth smells bad, and I start to get dizzy. I struggle for a minute before I fall to my knees, feeling powerless. The man catches me, throwing me over his shoulder before I black out completely.

***

When I regain consciousness, my head is pounding and my mouth feels dry. I slowly open my eyes and look around at the concrete walls around me and to the single door on the other side. I slowly stand up and stretch the stiffness out of my body.

I figure whoever took me has probably locked the door, but I might as well try it. I walk over, and like I thought, the door is locked. I sit back down in the corner and just stare at the wall thinking.

I wonder how long I have been gone and if James has noticed I'm missing. This will be the second time I am taken away from my family, and I don't know if I will make it out alive this time. I feel a tear go down my cheek at the thought of never seeing James again.

Then I feel something very foreign to me—anger. I am angry. I didn't ask for anything of this. I am a good person who deserves a happy life. Weren't those ten long years enough? Wasn't I tortured enough?

Why is this happening again?

Hours go by, and by the time I hear footsteps coming down the hall, I am furious. When the door opens and I look at the face of the people who walk through, the blood in my veins turns cold.

There stands my Aunt Molly with Kyle.

Kyle was one of the men who kept me in that little cabin for years; one of the men responsible for the despicable things that were done to me.

A man who I thought was dead.

"Aw, Gracie, don't look too surprised. I had to come back for my favorite brat," Kyle says with an arrogant grin stretching across his face.

"Kyle!" Molly snaps.

"Aw, babe, don't be jealous. You know I love you." He leans down and gives her a kiss. This man is in his thirties, and Molly is in her forties. I know they aren't mates because Dante's father died right after I was born. I never really met his dad, and Dante was too young to remember much about him.

They pull apart and look over to me.

"Well, I wish I could say I was sad that this is coming to an end, but your death is going to give me so much happiness." Molly claps her hands together.

"Why?" I whisper.

"Why? Because you ruined everything! Paul and your father had an agreement when your parents found out you were going to be a girl. They agreed to raise both of you and Dante to be alphas! Female alphas were practically unheard of so they would train both of you, and if you weren't strong enough or didn't want the job, it would go to Dante! But of course, you became strong and brave when you turned five. You would stick up for anyone at school, and you got into tussles with your classmates all the time if someone was being picked on. You showed signs of being a good leader early on, and we all saw that! You remember that?" She takes a deep breath, getting angrier with each sentence. "Paul died, but your father kept his word until you were six. Then he decided that without any help and with both of you getting older, he could only train one of you. And since you were the daughter of the alpha and with your so-called 'leading abilities,' he chose you. Dante could have had everything if it weren't for you!" She spits out at me.

"He did!" I yelled back finally. She wasn't the only one getting angrier. "Dante got everything! He got the Alpha position and the training. He got to go to school, and he got to meet his mate in a normal way! Don't you understand? He got a life! Something I never had! I never got to go to school. I never got to be with my family. I never got to complain about school work or training because I didn't have any of that! I had to be tortured and abused by the man standing right next to you!" I point to Kyle and take a deep breath, calming down after my outburst.

I could never be mad at Dante for getting those things and the title. He was family, and it wasn't his fault. I love him no matter what. I may be jealous that he got to have a normal life, but I could never hold that against him. I am sure that given a choice, he would have given it all up so none of this would have happened. No normal person would subject another to what I had been through for a title.

"You deserved everything that happened to you! You were a whiny little bitch! You didn't deserve the title!" she screamed back.

I look down at my bare legs and get furious. "Did I deserve these?" I point towards the inside of my legs, with tears in my eyes and my hoarse voice from screaming. I point to the inside of my thighs where there are scar versions of tic-tac-toe.

The second year I was there, and I was about ten, the guys had been doing unimaginable things to me for two years already. I suppose they ran out of ideas for a little bit and they were still trying everything to get me to talk again. They took the kitchen knives, strapped my arms and legs down to the table, and played tic-tac-toe using my skin as their paper and the knives as their pencils. The scars never healed.

I think back to when James first noticed them in the shower. I get angry again thinking she took me away from him. I should be with him right now. We should be going back to our pack and starting the rest of our lives together.

I start breathing heavily as my pulse increases. I watch as Molly stares at the scars. There is a slight trace of horror on her face.

"Did I deserve these too?" I scream and turn around, lifting up the back of my shirt to show the swirly patterns of scars that they used to carve into my back along with burn marks.

I drop my shirt and turn around. I am getting so angry; I swear I am seeing red. She just stands there dumbfounded. I hear a noise outside, and Kyle curses under his breath before running out the door. Molly just stands there.

"Do you have…?" I breathe heavily. "Anything." I let out another breath. "To say for yourself?" I scream the last part.

She straightens up and squares her shoulders. "Well, I told them to get rid of you, not keep you. Those are results of you being the little bitch that you are," she replies, smirking at me.

Whatever sense of self-control I had seconds before is completely gone. I can hear the noise of fighting and growling coming closer, but I don't care at this point.

"You should have died years ago," Molly screams before running towards me. She hits me head-on and knocks me back into the wall. I wince at the impact, but it doesn't affect me enough to keep me from going after her.

I thought maybe that once she knew what they really did, she would be at least a little bit sorry for being the cause of it. But to know that she still blames me for everything, I suddenly don't care if she lives or dies.

She is a terrible person.

I take in a deep breath before pushing back on her with all of my strength. I am surprised to find that I actually moved her back a couple of feet.

I charge at her before she can act, punching her in the face. She falls to the ground, and I am on her quickly. I land in another punch before she throws me off her and backs a couple of feet. I crumple to the ground, and right as she steps in front of my face, I grab her ankles and pull it, sitting up at the same time.

She falls back, and I can hear the crack of her skull on the cement floors. I don't know if that killed her, and I certainly don't care anymore.

I lay back down on the ground as I start to get strange pains in my body. I lie on the ground and stare at the ceiling while breathing heavily, trying to figure out what is going on.

I hear my name being called before I hear a distinct popping noise from my leg. An excruciating pain shoots up my body after. I scream out and look to see my leg at a weird angle. Seconds go by, and one by one, I can feel my bones shifting and starting to break. I know I am starting to shift.

"Grace!" I hear from the doorway. James runs in and dashes to my side, but right as he is about to pick me up, I feel my spine start twisting, and I scream out, writhing on the ground.

"Grace? Grace, what's wrong, baby?" I faintly hear him. I am too focused on the pain to answer.

A couple of minutes later, James is still trying to talk to me when I hear others walk into the room.

I am breathing heavily and screaming every time a bone breaks. I am trying to stop it, but it's like I have no control over it right now.

"...need to get her to complete the change. If she keeps resisting it, her body will not be able to heal all of the bones that have broken and all of her internal organs that have started shifting. She will die, James. I told you... risks... her changing... not strong enough...."

I think I hear Dr. Kelly, but the popping and roaring in my ears wash her voice out. My vision is blurring from all of the pain. I tune out a lot of the conversation and focus on my body, trying to stop it from what it's doing. I hear a pop closer to my face, and my shoulder is the next part to start burning with pain.

A second or two goes by before I hear James next to me.

"Baby, you got to let go. Stop fighting it and let it take over," James says, getting as close as he can without my spasms hitting him.

"I... can't." I breathe. "It... hurts," I whimper. Another scream comes up as I feel my left foot snap.

"Baby, let go. It hurts because you are fighting it. You need to let go. Embrace it! Think of yourself as a wolf. What do you think that would feel like? What would it be like to have paws and fur and be able to run fast as lightning?" He strokes my hair.

I stop writhing a second later and start picturing myself running alongside James. I start to imagine being able to run and play and shift just like everybody else.

The pain lessens, but I can feel my bones snapping now. It feels more like cracking a knuckle than breaking a bone. Minutes go by like this while

James continues to whisper encouraging things in my ear. Suddenly, I can start to feel my skin a bit tingly. I don't hear anymore snapping, and when I go to open my eyes, everything looks different.

I can see everything so much clearer and sharper. I look at James. His features are so defined, and I can clearly see the stubble on his jaw. I can see the worry across his face. I try to give him a smile, but I feel weird.

"Grace?"

A sudden wave of fatigue hits me, and I feel myself falling before I fell totally unconscious.

Chapter 31

I don't know what has happened to me. For a long time, I feel weightless, like I am drifting. I feel neither awake nor asleep. I am neither here nor there. This has been happening for so long that I can't keep track anymore. Sometimes I feel warmth and comfort, and there are short periods where that disappears.

All I know is that I look forward to whoever is holding my hand and feel the tingles that seem to go around my whole body.

".... still doing here? Your sister.... you. If anything changes... Grace... know immediately... she is fine."

That voice sounds so familiar, and I want to scream out that I'm not fine. That once the warmth disappears from my side, I would feel lost, like I am missing something.

After a while, I drift in and out, listening to the voices around me. The conversations seem to become clearer. I can finally make out a whole sentence of what they are saying.

I am tired of not knowing what's going on around me, and I desperately wish I could wake up. I want the warmth and the tingles back.

For the next couple of minutes, I focus on moving any part of my body that I can; move my hands or my toes, or maybe open my eyes or move my face. It takes a lot of effort, but I can feel my hand twitch.

I hear someone gasp and then grab my hand. They are warm, but it's not the person I am looking for.

"Grace? Honey, are you awake?"

I focus all of my energy and move one of my fingers. They gasp again. I hear a voice telling someone to get the doctor and James.

I try to open my eyes, but nothing works. I can feel people poking me and checking things. People ask me to move my hand or my toes, and I manage to move those couple of times, but each time takes a little more energy from me.

A little later, I feel someone grab my hand, and the warmth and the tingles return. This sends a little bit of energy through me. I want to open my eyes and see who this person is, but the more I try, the more frustrated I become.

"...princess. Come on. I know you can do it. Open your eyes. Let me see those beautiful eyes."

I feel something warm being pressed on my forehead. One of their hands is completely closed around mine while the other is stroking my hair. I try again, and I manage to get my eyes to crack open before the lights above me get too bright. I have to close them again.

"That's great, baby." Someone places a kiss on my forehead. "Can someone dim the lights a little?" He calls out behind him.

I try to open my eyes again, and when I look up, I see the most gorgeous man staring down at me.

"Hey, baby. How do you feel?"

I look at him. I then look around and see an older looking couple who looks so familiar and another couple; both couples have their arms around each other. They are all looking at me strangely. Next to them, I see a doctor in a white lab coat, and he has a clipboard in his hand.

"Grace? Do you know where you are?" the good-looking man asks.

"Not really." I manage to croak out. I see the older lady rush out the door and come back in with a bottle of water. I take it from her, giving her a small smile. I carefully take a sip, with the man helping to make sure I don't drop the bottle.

I look back over to him and back to the lady. She looks so familiar. Everyone around me looks so familiar that it's almost weird.

"Grace? Do you remember me? I'm Doctor Richards." The man in the white lab coat comes over to me, checking the monitors next to me. He flashes a light in my eyes.

Once he is done, I turn to the man on the other side of me. "Who are you?" I ask him.

The look of sadness that comes across his face is heartbreaking. He covers his face. I want to hug him, but I don't know if that's weird.

"Baby, do you know anyone in this room?" I look around at all the faces. They all look familiar, but I can't place them.

"No. I mean, I feel like I should know you, but I don't know why or how." I look around at everybody before looking down at my hands. "I'm sorry," I mumble.

"No, honey. Don't worry about it. We can tell you if you would like." The woman that got me the water comes over and holds my hand. I look from her to the beautiful man and nod my head.

"Before we tell you, is there anything at all that you remember? Do you remember anything about yourself or the world and anything that happened this past couple months? Anything you can remember will help, darling," she says, looking at me with kind eyes.

I look around at all of them again and think. I think as hard as I can before a headache starts forming. "Are you guys my family? I feel like I know all of you really well… a-and…" I stutter, looking back at the beautiful man.

"And what?" he asks with a hopeful look in his eyes.

"A-are we… t-together?" I ask, looking down at my hand in his, suddenly nervous. I hear him let out a breath of air before he chuckles.

"Yes, sweetie. We are together." He kisses my forehead, and I blush.

I look over to the woman. She has a smile on her face and grabs my hand. "Anything else?" she asks.

"Not really. I mean I think I know you, but I feel like I haven't seen you in a really long time."

She gets a small smile on her face before looking over to the older man next to her. "We are your parents, and the girl you see over there is your sister with her, uh, boyfriend. My name is Lilliana and your father over there is Leo. Your sister is Adeline, and that's Cole next to her. Do you know the man next to you?" she asks.

I look next to me and think about it. "Jay?" I ask. I think that's close.

"That's close enough, baby. My name is James," he says, tucking some more hair behind my ear. I nod my head.

"Why do I feel these warm tingles and warmth whenever you touch me?" I ask.

"Baby, there are a lot of things we have to explain, but I don't want to give you too much right now, okay? I promise over the next couple of days that we will explain everything. We'll do it one day at a time. You have had a bad accident, and you have been asleep for a while. We don't want to overwhelm you with so much information, "James says, looking at me intently. I nod my head and look around.

Everyone is looking at me with sad smiles, and I look to my sister. "Hi," I say. She looks at me and quickly walks over to my bed, giving me a warm hug.

This is going to be an interesting couple of days.

***

A few days later, I got to know more about myself. I have met a lot of my other friends again, and some of them I feel like I know, but others seem to be complete strangers. My parents and James explained that we live in this big community house, and that's why there are so many people around.

James hasn't explained how we met or anything yet, and he hasn't told me how I ended up in the hospital, but he says he will finish explaining everything he can after lunch today.

Right now, we are all eating lunch, and I'm talking to Adeline and her boyfriend, Cole, about the things Adeline and I used to do as kids. They have shown me albums from when I was a little kid and then more pictures from a couple of weeks ago. I have noticed that there is a huge gap from when I was about eight or nine until recently. Even then, there are only some recent pictures, and they look like they are all taken around the same time.

I look at myself in these pictures, and they seem familiar, but I can't recall the actual events.

After lunch, I help clean up before James leads me outside. The past couple of days, we have been talking a lot, and we sleep in the same bed. I am so comfortable around him for someone I don't remember, and I always feel safe in his arms, which isn't hard because I notice how tall he is compared to me. Everyone is actually taller than me. When I look at myself in the mirror, it feels like I recognize myself. I have also noticed all of the scars I have. Some scare me more than others, like the ones on my inner thighs.

I also noticed I have a tattoo with James' initials, so I guess we must have been together for a long time to have his initials tattooed on my body next to the moon. The red on the tattoo looks really cool though.

I look back and see my family, along with Hazel and Dave, who are some of my friends I feel closer with, following behind us. "What's going on, James?" I ask, a little uncertain.

He stops in the front yard and turns to me. "Do you trust me?" he asks, looking into my eyes.

"Of course," I answer, nodding my head.

"Please know that I would never hurt you. Your whole family is here for you no matter how you feel about all of this afterward. Nobody will ever hurt you, okay?" he says again, and I nod my head, feeling nervous.

"I'm not sure what's the best way to tell you this, so I'm just going to say it and show you, okay?" he asks, nervously. I nod at him. "Everyone in this community is the same. We live together because we all have something in common and we protect each other. We are all a family, including you and your family. We are all werewolves." He finishes, looking at me closely.

I nod my head, processing what he just said. "What does that mean?" I ask confused.

"We can turn into wolves whenever we want or when strong emotions take over, like fear or anger. I'm going to show you now, and please don't be scared. I would never hurt you, okay?" He looks at me hesitantly. I nod my head, and he takes his pants off then his shirt.

I quickly block my eyes. "What are you doing?" I yell.

He chuckles. "It's okay. I'm not naked. Just open your eyes, baby."

I look up and see that he is still in his boxers. He gives me one more smile before I see something starting to move under his skin. I watch his body closely and hear cracking. And just as quickly as it started, it's over, and standing before me is a huge black wolf.

I hold my breath, waiting for something to happen. I try and comprehend what is happening, but my mind is in complete chaos right now. I think James just turned into a wolf, but that's not possible.

That can't be possible.

I think I was holding my breath too long because I start to get dizzy and fall to my knees. I start breathing again, gasping for breath.

James turned into a wolf!

Not even a second after I fall to my knees, I feel a whoosh of air, and something furry is curled around me. I look around and see the wolf—or James—curled around me. His head is in front of me, staring at me as if waiting to see if I am going to fall.

I stare at his eyes that are the exact replica of James' chocolate brown ones. I also feel the warmth and the tingles everywhere his body is in contact with mine.

"W-what?" I ask breathlessly. James whines before putting his head down on his paws, still looking up at me.

I reach my hand out, and he lifts his head up. I don't know why this startles me, but as a reflex, I pull my hand back to myself the second he puts his head back up. He whines and puts his head down again and closes his eyes. I slowly reach my hand out again and pet the top of his head.

I stroke his head to his ears and down his back, staring at his beautiful and soft fur. I can hear him purring against my touch. I smile a little at the noise.

"James?" I ask. He lifts his head up and looks at me, tilting his head to the side. The gesture is so cute that I let out a small giggle. At this, his ears perk up a little more, and I swear he is giving me a wolfish smile. The next thing I know, he is leaning closer to me, and I feel something wet go up the side of my face.

"James! Did you just lick me?" I ask, shocked. He seems to be smiling again with his tongue hanging out the side.

I giggle and pull my legs out from under me and sit crisscross, leaning back into his body that surrounds me. He feels so warm and feels like my own small cocoon. The air is chilly, and when he sees me leaning into him, he circles me a little tighter, so his entire body is blocking as much wind as possible, warming me up.

I look back and see my family watching me closely. My friends, my parents, Adeline and her boyfriend, are all watching me, trying to gauge my reaction.

"Are you all like this?" I ask.

My mom nods and looks to my dad before speaking. "Yes, honey, everyone in the house, besides a few, is like this. We were born this way, and the community we live in is a pack. We protect each other and help each other," she says, giving me a smile. I nod, wondering why I am taking this so well.

"But am I not your daughter? Do I change like this too?" I ask, confused. Maybe this has something to do with why I have no memory.

"Yes, sweetie—" she begins.

"Sorry I'm interrupting, but James wants us to go inside, he said the cold won't be good for Grace," Cole says.

"Wait, James said that? How do you know?" I ask, looking between the two, confused.

"We can explain everything inside honey, but let's go," my dad says gently.

I nod before standing up. I look back down at James. Once he stands up, I realize how big his wolf actually is. It's bigger than a normal wild wolf, and his head is over my own. My head comes to about his shoulder.

"Do you have to become human again?" I ask quietly.

I can stay like this if you want, princess. I hear James' voice in my head.

I gasp. "How did you talk?"

It's one of the things I can do. It's how I was just talking to Cole; I can talk to you through our minds. Nobody else can hear us right now, baby. It's called a mind link. Everyone in the pack can do it.

He nudges my lower back with his head towards the house. I start walking on my own, and James falls into step beside me.

I walk into the house, following everyone into the living room.

Do you want to sit with me again? You are still cold. I can feel it, he tells me in my mind.

I nod.

Okay, grab one of the pillows and sit on it on the floor.

I do as he says, and he curls around me again. I lean back into his belly and lay my head on his shoulder.

Over the next hour, everybody does their best at explaining everything and answering my questions. They explain James found me after I was apparently missing for ten years. They don't tell me where I was, where my wolf went, or how James and I ended up together. James tells me in our minds not to ask because he will explain those things later.

Chapter 32

It's just about dinner time after my family and friends explain all they can to me. The ladies go into the kitchen to cook while James heads upstairs to put some clothes on. I sit at the counter in the kitchen, thinking over everything they have just told me.

We live in a pack, and supposedly, James is the leader, and I'm supposed to be too. How can I help lead if I know nothing about this life? How can I lead if I don't even have a wolf or I can't change into one? My head is spinning with all of the questions going through my mind.

James walks downstairs and slips an arm on the back of my chair and looks at me.

"You have a lot of questions, don't you?" he asks.

I nod, and he nods back. Next thing I know, he is swinging me up from the chair and into his arms.

"Hey, we are going to go to our room for the night. Grace is tired, and I will come down in a bit to make us dinner. You all can eat without us," he says to everyone in the kitchen. Everyone nods, looking at me and giving me small smiles.

We walk up the stairs like this and to our bedroom. He closes the door before he puts me on the bed and sits behind me, wrapping his arms around me and lacing our hands together.

"Okay, what's your first question?" he asks

"How did we meet?" I look behind me to look at his face.

"Some of the pack members found you in the woods, and I knew you were my mate," he says, looking sad at the memory.

Maybe he didn't want me as his mate, whatever that is.

"Baby, I can hear your thoughts. It's not that I didn't want you, I'm just sad with the way you were found. I'm going to explain as much as I know and you can ask me questions once I'm done. How about that?" he asks, looking at my face.

I nod, looking down and leaning back into his chest.

He tells me that he found me in the woods and that bad things had happened to me, but he wasn't sure if I wanted to hear those details yet. After going back to my pack and seeing my family again, there was an incident where I went missing again then tried to shift, which almost killed me.

"We asked the doctor, and he has no idea why your memory is gone. But he guessed that... when a person goes through some traumatic experiences, their mind has ways of trying to cope with everything. Everyone is different, but for some reason, when your wolf was dying, it took all of your memories of anything bad that ever happened to help you so you wouldn't have to deal with it anymore. Dr. Richards said if your wolf were there, she would have surfaced by now along with your memories. But my wolf can't feel yours. Before, he still could feel her dormant, now my wolf feels nothing. He is very distraught at losing his other wolf half but is glad the human half survived.

"Technically, my wolf and I are the same person but not at the same time. It's hard to explain. To him, having you alive at all is a blessing after everything that has happened. You still will have the wolf gene, but since she is gone, you are human now in all other ways. There have been similar cases like if a werewolf gets too much silver in their system or wolfsbane, but usually, they don't lose their memories, just their wolves." He finishes, looking at me sadly.

"What's a mate?" I ask shyly.

"It's short for soul mate. The person you are destined to be with. Everybody in the world has one, but as werewolves, we can identify ours once we come in contact with them just by looking them in the eyes. That's why you feel the warmth and tingles the way you do. The tingles are the mating pull, and the warmth is because my body is adjusting its temperature to be able to keep you warm. Now that you are human, your body can't regulate its temperature the way werewolves can. The doctor also thought this was a sign of your wolf being gone forever because every time you get cold, my body temperature goes up as the instinct to keep you, as my mate, warm and healthy. This happened when I first found you, but the stronger you got, the less my wolf felt like he needed to protect you. Now that you are human, he feels the need to do everything he can to protect you," he says, looking down at me while running a hand through my hair.

I nod, taking it all in. So he is my soul mate. I ask a couple more questions about the mind link and his other abilities before we go into silence. He is probably waiting for me to freak, not that I blame him. Any normal person would be, but hearing all of this just feels right, like I know in my heart that he is telling the truth; kind of like how I had the gut feeling that I knew him when I woke up.

"Hey, James?" I ask.

"Hmm?" he replies, pressing a kiss on the top of my head.

"Are you ever going to tell me who took me or why?" I ask hesitantly. I'm not sure if I want to know, considering it was bad enough that my wolf felt the need to take all of the memories related to it away.

"If you really believe you should know, I can tell you. You were scared, Grace, and you even said to me one time that you wished you had a normal life where you didn't have to worry about everything all the time. Sometimes, the saying 'ignorance is bliss' is right. I think it's better not to know, but if you really want to know, I can tell you. And if you change your mind six months or years from now, I can tell you then too. It's all up to you, baby," he says.

I nod my head and think it over. I have a chance to start a life with a clean slate, clear from the horrors of whatever happened to me. Would I be dumb if I didn't take it? Or would it be selfish of me to move on not caring about the past? It's in the past, and I wouldn't want it to impact any future I have with James.

"I guess I'll think about it. You can always tell me another time if I want, right?" I ask, turning around in his lap to face him.

"Of course, any time you want, princess," he says, kissing my forehead.

"I just wish I remembered all of the good times we had together. I want to remember those and remember the times I had with my family," I say, looking down dejectedly.

"I think I have an idea, babe. Don't get too excited because I'm not 100% sure how to do this. We were at a fire with your family, and you were thinking of the memories of you as a child, and using the mind link, you shared them with me," he says, bringing his hands to the sides of my face. "Just close your eyes and open your mind to me, baby. I'm going to try, okay?" he says.

I nod, and he gives me a quick peck before pulling back and closing his eyes. I close my eyes as well, and just like he says, I try and leave my mind as open as I can.

Images start flashing in front of me. A younger version of me is playing by a waterfall with a little boy. We are having a great time and splashing in the water. I can feel the water on my skin and hear the laughter coming from us almost like I am there. I gasp and pull back, opening my eyes and looking at James in front of me.

"Did it work?" he asks skeptically.

"Yes, do you have more memories?" I ask eagerly. He chuckles before nodding.

"Yes, I do." He brings his hands back to my face.

I close my eyes with him, and before I know it, more images from my childhood with my family and these two other kids flash around before my eyes. I learn Adeline is one, along with Dante being the other. I think I remember someone mentioning him being my cousin and he is the mate of James' sister.

The memories go from me being a child and skip forward about ten years. This time, I am with James. We are in a hospital room, and I am on the bed, coloring with a little girl and Hazel. James is watching from the doorway for a couple of minutes before he speaks, and I can feel the love and concern he already had for me.

The next memory shows me with James in a bathroom. I realize we are in a bathtub, splashing around and laughing. In this, I have longer hair, and I appear to have a few scrapes and bruises.

Another memory of James walking in and seeing me with the hair cut I have now flows to my mind. Pure adoration is in his eyes at seeing me.

The next one is the time James gave me his bear. *You are my other half and my soul mate, and I love you. I always have and I always will, no matter what we go through together.*

The next one is my family in a hospital room, and watching us all hug while I'm sitting on the bed, is James. I don't know what happened, but that would be the second time I was in a hospital bed.

He goes to another memory of us walking outside at night with our *arms around each other.*

"What's wrong, baby?" he asks, cupping my face.

"Nothing," I say, tears forming in my eyes—not the sad kind but the happy kind, knowing that I get to spend the rest of my life with this man.

"Baby, please," he whispers. He looks so worried with his brow all scrunched up. I reach my hands up and pull them out of my sleeves. With my thumb, I run it along with his brow and give him a small smile.

"I love you."

I watch it all unfold as I tell James exactly how I feel about him and everything amazing about him.

He weaves his arms around my waist and picks me up, spinning me around. I giggle as I bury my head in his shoulder. He places me on the ground, and one of his hands comes up to rest on the side of my face, his thumb caressing my cheek.

"You have no idea how much you mean to me. I love you so much, baby." He pulls me in for another kiss. This time a slower, more passionate one.

I smile and open my eyes at the memories. The more he shows me, the more I remember them from my perspective, not the third person view of it.

I smile while a lone tear goes down my face. I lean in to kiss him. He kisses me back, and before I know it, we are wrapped up in each other with not a care in the world.

I know it will be a long road to a normal life for me, whatever that normal may be. But I don't need to know about my past right now because I know my future is with James, wherever the future takes us.

Can't get enough of James and Grace? Make sure you sign up for the author's blog to find out more about them!

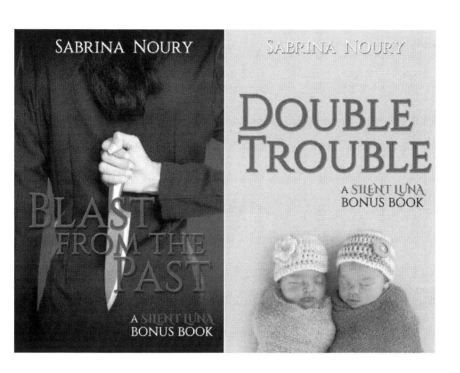

Get these two bonus chapters and more freebies when you sign up at sabrina_noury@awesomeauthors.org

Here is a sample from another story you may enjoy:

FIGHTING BLIND

E. MARIE

Chapter 1

I could hear the quiet crunch of grass beneath his feet, smell the salty sweat coming from the other nervous wolves around us, and taste the bitter-sweetness of the alpha's confidence. It was intoxicating.

I inhaled deeply and felt myself relax even further, a knowing smile on my lips as the wolf charged at me. I kept still, waiting it out until the last second had almost passed too late. When I did move, it was when I could feel his warm breath on my cheek as he snarled, the heat of his body searing onto mine.

With reflexes that never ceases to surprise even me, I sidestepped while subtly sticking my foot out as he whizzed past me. A second later, I heard his body thump against the ground. I chuckled as I heard gasps surround us. Their reactions were pretty predictable at this point. I'd visited many packs, and I could practically play out all of their reactions by now. The wolf before me snarled loudly, probably flashing his canines at me. I rolled my eyes. Too bad it wouldn't intimidate me.

"Come on, I don't have all day." I huffed with impatience that seemed to spur him on as he jumped and changed in midair. I watched as the air rippled around the colorful mass, and I mean ripple. I could see how it seemed to shimmer before the mass in front of me became larger. Judging by the way the air rippling around him, I could see he was a decent-sized wolf but nothing I couldn't handle.

Letting out one loud growl, he charged once more. I quickly went into a defensive position and prepared for the impact. He was a lot heavier than I had predicted as he slammed into me with full force. Letting out a grunt, I wrapped my arms around his neck tightly while I was pushed back several feet. I heard the snap of his teeth as he tried to bite my face off while his body trembled violently with his growls.

"Dear Goddess, you need to lose weight." I gritted out before falling down onto my back, using this momentum to kick the wolf over my head. He whined from the impact, but I didn't give him a chance to recover as I stood and kicked him in the stomach. He yelped, and I knew just from the sound of a crack, I had broken a couple of his ribs. I jumped back to let him recover for a few seconds, his heavy pants filling the silent air around us.

He snarled viciously, and I yawned in return before shooting him a wide grin. He circled me all the while snapping towards me every few seconds; testing the waters, I presumed.

I almost ended it, as I was starting to get incredibly bored, but he decided to kick the excitement up a notch. As he jumped towards me a second time, he surprised me by changing back into his human form and tackled me to the ground. He elbowed me in the gut, knocking the air out of my lungs.

He straddled my waist as he threw a punch to my right cheek. My head whipped sharply to the side, and I felt my sunglasses fly off somewhere. Pain flared on my face but instantly dimmed and went away. I laughed once I was hit again. I felt his body freeze above me, and the sharp intake of his breath told me he caught sight of my eyes. I stared straight up at him, a grin once again on my face.

"Good job, pup. Not only did you land one but two punches. You managed to surprise me. I gotta say I'm impressed." I grinned wickedly. "But sadly, I must end the fun."

"What are you—" He was cut off by his own grunt as I threw my own punch, a solid right hook might I add. His weight was lifted off me, and I jumped to my feet without a moment to spare, crouching low. He let out a groan before I noticed his outline showing him stumbling to his feet.

I attacked him one last time, running at him and jumping, my feet landing on his chest with a solid thump. His body flew back several feet, hitting what sounded like a tree. I noticed his colors dim, meaning he was unconscious. If he were dead, there would be a lifeless, dull gray, and the smell of death would reek throughout the air. Nodding in satisfaction, I brushed my hands together as if dusting them off and turned to look at the silent crowd. Gasps and soft curses surrounded me, and the color orange of surprise zinging around me. The bright color held my attention until a booming voice brought me out of my reverie.

"Take him to the pack doctor."

"Yes, Alpha," a couple men responded instantly. I saw their colorful figures picking him up and hurrying him away. I turned to face the alpha and noticed the color orange mix in with his power. I smirked once I saw it. I guess even the big, bad alpha could be surprised.

"What are you?" he demanded. I lifted my hand to run through my hair but was surprised to see my hood was still up. Wow, that was magic all on its own.

"I'm a werewolf," was my short reply.

"But what else?" I shrugged and made the show of darting my eyes around before landing back onto him.

"I think it's best told in private." He was quietly debating my answer, and I was waiting once again.

"How about you pull off that hood to show your face more clearly?" He rumbled, and I shrugged.

"Fine, not like I'm hiding my identity, anyway." Reaching up, I pushed my hood back to reveal my face. I felt my hair roll over my shoulders and down my back. More orange colored my vision, my appearance surprising everyone around me, unsurprisingly. I felt my hair spill over my shoulders and down my back. I've asked many people about my appearance; as I became blind when I was young, my memories too faded for me to remember what I looked like. From what they described, I had shifting eyes that would change between the colors bright emerald and ruby red, with a head of silver hair that looked as if the moon poured its silvery light onto the strands itself. Of course, I also joked that they were implying that I was the Moon Goddess, which is sort of a religious figure in werewolf standards. However, she is not an all-powerful being like the one the humans have with their God. The Moon Goddess is simply the first female werewolf to ever be created, along with her mate. But that's a story for another day.

"You are not only werewolf." His voice brought me out of my thoughts, and I gave him a wolfish smile.

"Like I said, let's talk in private." And with confident strides, I walked passed him and everybody else. Displaying a sure step and a cocky smirk, I knew he would follow. And he did.

If you enjoyed this sample then look for
Fighting Blind

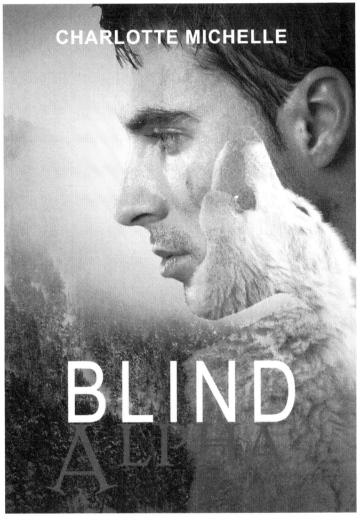

Other books you might enjoy:

King of Beasts

Jamiee Lynne

Available on Amazon!

Introducing the Characters Magazine App

Download the app to get the free issues of interviews from famous fiction characters and find your next favorite book!

iTunes: bit.ly/CharactersApple
Google Play: bit.ly/CharactersAndroid

Acknowledgements

To my editor and my agent and others who helped me with Silent Luna. You guys have answered every single one of my questions and helped me through this process when I had no idea what I was doing. This was a new experience for me and I don't know what I would have done without the constant emails and help you gave me.

A big thank you to all of my fans and followers who have read and been apart of the journey from the beginning. None of this would be possible if all of you hadn't voted and supported Silent Luna and me as a writer. All of the positive messages I get from all of you inspires me to keep going after my dreams.

To my boyfriend and best friend who has always encouraged me to do what makes me happy, no matter what. You talked me through a lot of doubting and second guessing myself and this book, and I will forever be grateful.

To my mom, who has always been a constant supporter and my rock to lean on when things get hard. There are not enough words to show how appreciative I am of you and everything you do for me.

To my dad who always believes in me and lifts me up when I doubt myself. You always talk about the future and the endless possibilities for me, and that makes me hopeful that anything is possible.

To Jeremy and Alicia, for never making life boring.

Author's Note

Hey there!

Thank you so much for reading *Silent Luna* I can't express how grateful I am for reading something that was once just a thought inside my head.

I'd love to hear from you! Please feel free to email me at sabrina_noury@awesomeauthors.org and sign up at sabrina-noury.awesomeauthors.org for freebies!

One last thing: I'd love to hear your thoughts on the book. Please leave a review on Amazon or Goodreads because I just love reading your comments and getting to know YOU!

Whether that review is good or bad, I'd still love to hear it!

Can't wait to hear from you!

Sabrina Noury

About the Author

Sabrina Noury was raised in New Hampshire. She graduated from Campbell High School in 2015, after being a part of the school's cheerleading team and baseball team as a manager. After graduation, Sabrina pursued her dream of publishing at Hofstra University, where she is working towards her Bachelor of Arts in English, with a Concentration in Publishing and Editing. She will graduate from Hofstra University in 2019.

Printed in Poland
by Amazon Fulfillment
Poland Sp. z o.o., Wrocław